P9-CQB-031

J.Albert Adams
Academy Media Center

THE
AWAKENING

QUANTUM PROPHECY

THE
AWAKENING

MICHAEL CARROLL

01

PHILOMEL BOOKS

PHILOMEL BOOKS

a division of Penguin Young Readers Group

Published by The Penguin Group

Penguin Group (USA) Inc., 375 Hudson Street, New York, NY 10014, U.S.A.

Penguin Group (Canada), 90 Eglinton Avenue East, Suite 700, Toronto, Canada M4P 2Y3

(a division of Pearson Penguin Canada Inc.)

Penguin Books Ltd, 80 Strand, London WC2R 0RL, England.

Penguin Ireland, 25 St. Stephen's Green, Dublin 2, Ireland

(a division of Penguin Books Ltd).

Penguin Group (Australia), 250 Camberwall Road, Camberwall, Victoria 3124, Australia

(a division of Pearson Australia Group Pty Ltd).

Penguin Books India Pvt Ltd, 11 Community Centre, Panchsheel Park, New Delhi – 110 017, India.

Penguin Group (NZ), Cnr Airborne and Rosedale Roads, Albany, Auckland 1310,

New Zealand (a division of Pearson New Zealand Ltd).

Penguin Books (South America) (Pty) Ltd, 24 Sturdee Avenue, Rosebank,

Johannesburg 2196, South Africa.

Penguin Books Ltd, Registered Offices: 80 Strand, London WC2R 0RL, England.

Copyright © 2006 by Michael Carroll.

First American Edition published in 2007 by Philomel Books,

a division of Penguin Young Readers Group, 345 Hudson Street, New York, NY 10014.

Philomel Books, Reg. U.S. Pat. & Tm. Off.

Published in Great Britain by HarperCollins Children's Books, London.

The scanning, unloading and distribution of this book via the Internet or via

any other means without the permission of the publisher is illegal and punishable by law.

Please purchase only authorized electronic editions, and do not participate in

or encourage electronic piracy of copyrighted materials.

Your support of the author's rights is appreciated.

The publisher does not have any control over and does not assume any responsibility

for author and third-party websites or their content.

Published simultaneously in Canada. Printed in the United States of America.

Design by Marikka Tamura. Text set in Calisto

Library of Congress Cataloging-in-Publication Data

Carroll, Michael Owen, 1966–

Quantum prophecy : the awakening / Michael Carroll.—1st American ed. p.   cm.

Summary: Ten years after the disappearance of superhumans—both heroes and villains—

thirteen-year-olds Danny and Colin begin to develop super powers, making them

the object of much unwanted attention.

[1. Heroes—Fiction.   2. Adventure and adventurers—Fiction.   3. Science fiction.]   I. Title.

PZ7.C23497Qua   2007   [Fic]—dc22   2006020993

ISBN 978-0-399-24725-5

1   3   5   7   9   10   8   6   4   2

First American Edition

To the staff and pupils—past, present, and future—
of St. Thomas' National School,
Jobstown, Dublin

Renata Soliz stood in the center of the empty field, directly in the path of the approaching figure.

She had her long black hair tied back and was wearing gray jeans and a plain red T-shirt. The only thing that marked her out as anything other than a normal girl was a pair of thick leather gloves and the black Zorro mask she'd "borrowed" from her little brother.

The midday sun broke through the clouds and illuminated the tall man making his way toward her.

Renata stood her ground, watching him approach.

Though Dioxin was still twenty meters away, there was a stench of death about him: a putrid, damp, fungal smell that reminded Renata of the rotting timbers in the basement of her grandmother's house. He sneered at her as he stomped forward over the rough ground, his grin spreading across the blotched yellow and red skin of his face like an opening wound. "Haven't you got the sense to run away, little girl?"

He continued walking toward her, the grass dying where his bare feet touched it.

Renata watched him carefully. She knew all about Dioxin, knew what he could do. His skin oozed a thick, clear, acidlike venom, and if his touch didn't scorch the flesh from your bones, it infected you with a deadly poison.

Dioxin stopped a couple of meters away. "Seriously. Run away."

Energy had told Renata that of all the villains she had faced, the one who scared her most was Dioxin. Ragnarök was incredibly intelligent, strong and fast; Brawn was four meters tall and capable of knocking a moving train clear off its tracks; Slaughter was a ruthless killing machine; but they were *nothing* compared with Dioxin.

"So what do they call you?" Dioxin sneered.

"Diamond."

Dioxin looked her up and down. "What's the deal here, kid? Don't tell me that *you're* one of Titan's crew! You're what, fifteen?"

"Fourteen."

"Fourteen. And you think you can stop *me*?"

With that, Dioxin lunged toward her, his poisonous arms outstretched.

Paragon quickly checked the information that was projected onto the inside of his visor. Flight power was down to less than forty percent.

A plasma bolt hit him in the left shoulder, burning a hole into his armor. He dodged to the right, quickly unclipped the still-burning shoulder pad and let it fall to the ground. A deep red welt appeared on his dark skin. One of the few active superheroes who didn't have any superhuman abilities, Paragon relied on his armor and weapons as much as his natural intelligence and athletic abilities, but there were times when even these weren't enough.

Paragon was sweating—and it wasn't just from the weight of his armor, or the heat of the plasma bolts.

This was a bad situation.

There had been no sign of Ragnarök for months and now this: a hundred-meter-long mobile fortress, rumbling its way across Pennsylvania toward the city of New York. The tank stopped for nothing; cars, trees and even houses were crushed beneath its giant wheels. Unable to halt or even slow the machine's progress, the police and army had concentrated on evacuating people from its path.

Another volley of plasma bolts streaked toward him and Paragon cut the power to his jetpack and dropped, angling his descent so that he was falling directly into the path of the enormous battle-tank.

He reactivated his jetpack ten meters above the ground and found himself face-to-face with Ragnarök, protected by the battle-tank's meter-thick windshield.

They stared at each other for a split second, then Ragnarök frantically gestured to one of his henchmen, mouthing the words, "Kill him!"

The armored hero dodged to his left just as a huge column of white flame scorched the air around him.

He swooped down toward the battle-tank's undercarriage, settled long enough to attach the explosive charge and then zoomed away, dodging a storm of bullets and plasma bolts.

Paragon glanced around. He could see Energy floating above the battle-tank, using her powers to deflect the tank's fire away from the others. Paragon activated the communicator built into his helmet. "Everyone! Pull back! Three seconds!"

There was a flurry of activity as the assembled superheroes darted to a safe distance, then—

The sound of the explosion was almost unnoticeable over the roar of the tank's massive engines, but everyone felt it; the ground trembled, the blast rattling windows for ten kilometers in every direction.

Paragon peered through the huge column of smoke and dust. He activated his visor's infrared filters and . . . Yes! The tank was burning!

"All right, people!" Paragon said. "Maybe the big guy isn't with us, but it looks like we've just had our first break. Max?"

Max Dalton's voice said, "I'm here, Paragon."

"Get inside the thing. See if you can lock on to someone."

"Will do."

"Energy, follow him. You might need to shield him against weapons-fire."

"Will do," Energy said.

"Quantum?"

Silence.

Paragon paused. "All right. We'll have to do it without him. Anyone know how Diamond is holding up?"

Dioxin raged. He ranted. This was *impossible*!

He'd reached out to infect her and the girl—Diamond—had simply locked her hands around his wrist and changed.

It had taken less than a second; she had shimmered, glistened and become solid, unmoving and transparent. Even her hair and clothes had changed. It was as though she'd been replaced with a statue carved out of solid diamond.

Dioxin couldn't shake her off. She wasn't movi
think that she *could* move in this form. All she wa
holding on to his wrist, still staring at him with that
look on her face.

A voice called out, "Dioxin!"

He turned to see an annoyingly familiar figure behind him.

Dioxin sighed. "Dalton."

Joshua Dalton smiled. "You can let go now, Diamond."

As Dioxin watched, the girl instantly turned back to normal.
She let go of his wrist, jumped backward and ripped the leather
gloves from her hands. She tossed the gloves aside. Even before
they hit the ground they were a smoldering ruin.

"See, the trouble with your power, Dioxin, is that you can't
even lift weights to build up some muscle, can you?" Joshua Dalton said. "No, you'd just burn through the bars. Now me, on the
other hand . . . Well, I'm not that strong either, certainly not compared with Titan. But a psychokinetic doesn't *need* to be strong."

Dioxin felt a sickening lurch in the pit of his stomach, then
looked down to see that he was floating a meter above the
ground, unable to do anything but wait to be arrested.

High above the battle-tank, Energy concentrated on drawing the
enemy fire toward her. Tiny flashes of blue and orange lightning
crackled around Energy's body and through her short auburn
hair. Her eyes—normally a pale gray—were now almost solid
white.

She knew that she could absorb a huge amount of power, but
there was a limit. Pretty soon now she'd have to discharge
that power.

. voice crackled over her communicator. "Energy? I'm on
.ne way!"

"Titan! Thank God! Where are you?"

"Just crossing the East Coast. I'll be there in a minute,"
Titan replied.

"Make it quicker! We're not doing well here. I'm trying to
pull in all their plasma bolts, but it hurts. I've never seen so
much firepower!"

"I see you!"

Energy looked to the east and Titan was suddenly hovering
in front of her, his dark blue cape billowing in the light breeze.
"Don't just float there! *Do* something!" she told him.

"Yes, ma'am!"

Titan gave her a quick smile, then darted down to the battle-
tank.

Shots blasted into him, missiles exploding to his left and right.
It was as though the battle-tank had been designed with the sole
purpose of hurting him—and it was doing a pretty good job.

Titan was strong and fast, but he wasn't invulnerable. When
he was hit, he felt it. And he was being hit a lot right now. Soon
his chest was a mass of bruises and his costume—bright blue
tunic and leggings, darker blue cape, gloves and boots—started
to get more holes than a fishing net. Much more of this and he'd
be flying around in his underpants.

Through the tank's meter-thick windscreen, Titan could see
Ragnarök at the controls, ordering his men about. The madman
had a determined look on his face. That wasn't unusual for someone like him; they *all* believed in what they were doing.

Where the hell is Quantum? he wondered. *He should be here by now! He'd be able to phase himself* inside *the tank! And what about Max? Why hasn't he been able to reach someone on the inside of it? Could Ragnarök have found a way to shield the tank from Max's mind control?*

Titan looked again at Ragnarök. The villain was looking determined, but not concerned.

There's something else happening here. What is Ragnarök planning?

For the first time in years, Titan was genuinely worried.

Diamond stood on a low hill, some way from the main battle. Ahead, she could see Ragnarök's battle-tank as it rumbled onward.

The tank had left a channel of destruction as far as she could see.

"It's huge," Diamond said. "Energy said it was big, but I didn't think . . . Josh, how can we possibly stop something like this?"

He hesitated. "I don't know. Look, Diamond . . . You shouldn't have to face this. Not yet. I'm going to leave you here. Somewhere safe. OK?"

"No! *Not* OK! You can't just leave me out of it!"

"This is your first battle."

Diamond stared into Joshua Dalton's eyes. "I can take care of myself! I'm invulnerable! And I'm strong! A lot stronger than *you* are!"

"Physically, yes." He glanced past her, to the battle that was raging. "Emotionally, you're not ready. You stay put, Diamond. That's an order. Got that?"

She nodded.

"Good." Joshua Dalton leaned forward and kissed her gently on the forehead. "Wish me luck."

Max Dalton's power, like that of his younger brother Joshua and sister Roz, was mental rather than physical; he could temporarily take over the minds of anyone within a twelve-meter radius.

Max and his siblings were always easy to spot, even on this crowded battlefield; the members of The High Command were the only superheroes who didn't wear masks. All they wore were matching black Kevlar uniforms.

Now, as he ran across the battleground toward Paragon, he was glad of the fact that his costume was bulletproof.

Max helped Paragon to his feet. "You OK?"

The armored hero coughed and spat out a mouthful of blood. "I will be. Thanks. How are we doing?"

"Not good," Max replied. "Titan can't get close enough to the tank to do any damage. I've no idea where Quantum is. Impervia and Brawn are locked in a stalemate. Apex is down; The Glyph got him. The others . . . I'm losing track of them." Half an hour earlier, Max had seen the five members of Portugal's *Podermeninas* team battling dozens of Ragnarök's henchmen. Since then, there had been no sign of them.

"Max, I don't mind telling you . . . I'm scared," Paragon said. "I don't think we're all going to make it. If we can't stop that machine . . ."

"We *will* stop it."

"How? We've thrown everything we have at it and it's still going."

Max Dalton bit his lip. "I know. Listen, I passed something on the way back to you. It's . . . I think it was Thalamus. I think he's de—"

Max spun away, his hand clutching his neck. Blood dripped between his fingers.

Paragon grabbed Max's free arm and dragged him to the relative safety of a fallen tree.

"Let me see it," Paragon said. He pulled Max's blood-covered hand away and inspected the wound. "You'll be fine—I've had worse shaving cuts."

He removed a large bandage from his med-pack and pressed it against the wound. "This'll help for the time being, and we can get it looked at properly when this is all over."

"Thanks." Max grabbed Paragon's shoulder and hauled himself to his feet.

Paragon said, "What we need right now is a miracle." He paused. "Or, to be more accurate, we need—Quantum!"

"Exactly."

"No, I mean . . . he's here!"

Max Dalton and Paragon ran toward the battle-tank. Quantum, the fastest superhuman of them all, could not be seen, but there was no doubt that he was there. Ragnarök's henchmen were being knocked about by some invisible force, their weapons ripped from their hands, their armor torn off.

"Quantum, where the hell *were* you?" Paragon shouted as they neared the tank.

The white-clad superhero suddenly appeared in front of him, slightly out of breath. "I . . . I don't know. Something happened to me. How badly are we doing?"

Max said, "We have some dead and a few missing. We thought you were one of them. Look, we need Impervia to help Titan, so you've got to take on Brawn. You feel up to it?"

"Sure. Yeah. I can slow him down at least."

Paragon shook his head. "No, wait. Quantum, use that intangibility trick of yours; get inside the tank and see what damage you can do. At the very least, try and take out Ragnarök."

"OK," Quantum said, nodding. "I'll—" He shuddered. "Something's wrong." He looked down at his gloved hands. They were shaking. "I . . . I don't seem to be able to move."

Paragon exchanged a quick glance with Max. "What is it?" Paragon asked.

"I . . . Wait! There's a sense of . . . There's a machine; it's dangerous to us. Ragnarök's been used . . ." Quantum blinked rapidly, swaying back and forth. "Paragon? You're older."

Quantum's knees buckled and he collapsed.

Paragon reached out and caught him, then turned to Max, who was staring at Quantum. "Don't just stand there, Max! I'll look after Quantum. You get to Brawn—maybe *you* can control him."

Max hesitated. "No, it's never worked on him before."

"Damn it, Max! You have to *try!*"

Paragon watched Max go, then looked down at Quantum. "You still conscious?"

Quantum's eyes rolled back. "Paragon . . ." His voice was weak, barely a whisper.

"I'm here."

"When the boy comes to you, you have to believe him. You won't want to, but you must."

"What boy? What are you talking about?"

Quantum smiled. "He will be strong. That's how you'll know."

He reached out and grabbed Paragon's hand. "You've been a good friend." Then, in a stronger voice, he added, "Next, we lose. We *all* lose. Paragon, don't tell the others. Promise me."

"I promise," Paragon said. "I won't say a word. But I don't know what you're talking about."

"You will, Paragon. Not for a long time, but you will."

1

IT WAS A THURSDAY IN OCTOBER, EARLY afternoon. Normally at this time, Colin Wagner would be hiding behind the boy sitting in front of him, because Thursday afternoons were what his teacher liked to call "Discussion Time." This was when Mr. Stone would pick a topic he found interesting and do his very best to make sure that none of the students would ever find it interesting again.

The previous week, Mr. Stone had shown them a five-minute video about how birds build their nests and then proceeded to lead the class in a discussion about birds, nests and why he believed that starlings were more evil than magpies. But today, for a change, Mr. Stone had picked an interesting topic.

Today they were talking about Mystery Day.

Mr. Stone waited until everyone had settled down. "So . . . Tomorrow is Mystery Day," he began. "Exactly ten years since the disappearance of all the superheroes. When this all started, nine years ago on the first anniversary, it was supposed to be a day of remembrance. But somehow over the years it's turned into a bloody holiday! Instead of the heroes being honored for giving up their lives, we get balloons and parties, and people setting up stalls at the side of the road to sell knockoff Titan action figures and T-shirts."

He picked up his chalk and began to write on the blackboard. *Titan,* he wrote, and underlined it twice. *Poder-meninas,* he wrote next, but he underlined that only once. He followed that with a series of other names: *Paragon, Apex, Impervia, Thalamus, Thunder, Inferno, Energy, Quantum* and *Zephyr*.

Then he picked up his red chalk and wrote *Ragnarök*. Underneath that he wrote *Rayboy, The Glyph, Terrain, The Shark, Slaughter, Dioxin* and *Brawn*.

"Right . . ." Mr. Stone turned around to face the classroom. "Superheroes," he said, pointing to the words written in white. "And supervillains." He tapped at the words in red. "Who were they? Where did they come from? Where did they get their powers?"

"Nobody knows, sir," Colin said.

"Weren't the powers inherited?" Brian McDonald suggested.

"That would certainly explain The High Command: Max, Josh and Roz Dalton," Mr. Stone said.

Malcolm O'Neill put up his hand. "I heard they all came from another planet."

"Speculation," Mr. Stone said. "Pure speculation. Let's just stick to the facts, shall we? Their capabilities—their powers and strengths. Titan, who could fly and had the strength of a hundred men. Energy, who had the ability to absorb and then release almost any kind of energy. It was said Quantum could move so fast he was able to outrun a supersonic jet. But then ten years ago at least twenty-five superheroes and upward of a hundred villains were involved in a battle just east of Pittsburgh. Ragnarök's huge battle-tank caused massive destruction as it rumbled toward New York City. Three whole towns had to be evacuated. There are reports of a huge explosion and then . . . nothing. So what happened to the superheroes? Colin?"

"They disappeared, sir," Colin answered.

The teacher nodded. "Disappeared. Vanished. Where to? Danny?"

"Nobody knows," Danny Cooper replied. "But it wasn't just the *heroes* who disappeared. The villains did too. There weren't any bodies found in the wreckage. It was probably all covered up by the government."

"They went back to their home planet," Malcolm O'Neill said.

Adam Gilmore laughed. "Give it a rest, Mal! They were probably just vaporized in the explosion!"

"They can't have been," Colin said. "Brawn or Impervia would have survived any explosion. Energy could have absorbed the blast. Quantum could have just outrun it."

"Right," Danny Cooper said. "And Max Dalton and the rest of The High Command survived."

"Yeah, but they weren't *there*," Adam said.

"Mr. Gilmore raises an interesting point," Mr. Stone said. "Despite what some witnesses claim, the official word is that the Daltons were not present during the attack. As far as we know, they are the *only* superhumans to have survived Mystery Day. Every other superhuman—whether or not they were present during Ragnarök's attack—has disappeared." He shrugged. "Tonight Max Dalton will give his first interview in ten years. The first time he's ever spoken in public since he retired." The teacher walked around to the front of his desk and leaned back against it. "Anyone want to guess what he's going to say?"

Brian turned around to look at Malcolm O'Neill. "Hey, Mal! Maybe he's going to tell us that he's going to take you back to *your* home planet!"

The class laughed. "Right, Brian. . . ," Mr. Stone said. "You've just won the right to set today's homework for the rest of the class."

"Seriously?"

"Why not?"

Brian glanced around the room. Every other boy was staring at him with the same expression, doing their best to send Brian the same telepathic message: make this easy on us or you're a dead man!

Under his breath Colin muttered, "No homework! No homework!"

The teacher said, "Mr. McDonald?"

"I think that for our homework we should all have a good think about what it would have been like to be a superhero."

"A good think?"

"Yep," Brian said, nodding vigorously.

"Perfect. You all have a good think about it and then, when you're done thinking, write down those thoughts in the form of an essay."

Everyone groaned. Someone shouted, "Oh, well done, Brian!"

"It won't be that bad," Mr. Stone said. "There's no school tomorrow, so you have a three-day weekend in which to get it done. Four pages should be enough. And I want normal-sized paper too! No more essays written on bloody Post-it notes!"

Colin, Danny and Brian lived in different areas of the town, and every day they followed the same "going home" ritual; they would walk together until they reached the northwest corner of the park, then Colin would go east, Danny would go north to the apartment blocks and Brian would go west. As always, however, they spent an hour or so sitting on the low wall, chatting, arguing and watching out for flash cars or good-looking girls.

It was while they were doing this, sheltering from the rain under the park's enormous pine trees that overhung the path, that Brian spotted his younger sister approaching on her bike, doing her best to cycle around the puddles.

"Hey, here comes your girlfriend, Danny," Brian said.

"Oh, ha ha," Danny replied.

They watched as Susie wobbled her way toward them and stopped right in front of Danny. "Hi, Danny!"

Danny muttered a greeting, but deliberately avoided looking her in the eye.

"What do *you* want?" Brian asked her.

"Mummy says you're to come home now and stop dawdling."

"Does she really?"

"Yes."

Brian thought about this. "OK . . . I'll race you. You on the bike and me running."

Susie wasn't about to pass up an opportunity to show off in front of Danny. "OK then."

"I'll even give you a head start," Brian said. "I'll let you get as far as the end of the road."

She eyed him suspiciously. "No. You'll cheat or something."

Brian tried to look innocent. "Cheat? Me? Never! Danny will vouch for me, won't you, Dan?"

"Sure," Danny said reluctantly.

With that, Susie tore off down the road, pedaling like mad.

Brian watched her go. "Sucker." He turned to the others. "Pretty cool about the homework, isn't it? A lot better than math or geography."

"Couldn't you have come up with something easier?" Colin asked.

"It wasn't my fault! I didn't think he'd make us do an essay!"

"I'm going to pick Thalamus," Danny said. "He's my third favorite after Titan and Paragon."

"So why not do Paragon, then?" Brian asked.

"Because he's *everyone's* second favorite. What about you?"

"Thunder."

Danny laughed. "He's the one with the dumbest powers! Power over rain! What use is that? You never hear stories about how he managed to use his abilities to do *anything* other than make a loud bang or cause a sudden downpour! Why not pick Apex? He was pretty cool."

"Yeah, but no one knows much about him," Colin said.

"That's what makes him a good choice."

Brian said, "Well, maybe *you* think that Thunder is a bad choice, Danny, but I've got a few ideas to make it work. Who are you going to choose, Col?"

Colin shrugged. "I don't know . . . I'll probably end up forgetting again and doing it when I'm having my breakfast on Monday morning." He grinned. "I seem to work better when my dad is standing in front of me telling me over and over that I shouldn't put things off until the last minute."

"You could always write it from the point of view of one of the villains," Brian suggested.

Danny raised his eyes in disgust. "Brian, you're a moron! He said we have to write about one of the *heroes,* didn't he?"

"Yeah, he did. But look at it like this . . . Suppose that, say, Ragnarök *thought* that he was a hero."

Colin looked up at this. "Yeah, he always believed he was doing the right thing."

Danny nodded. "That's true, but let's face it, Ragnarök was a complete nutter. How the hell could robbing banks and holding the world to ransom be anything but the work of a villain? If you do evil things you're still evil—no matter what the reason."

They fell silent as they spotted a quartet of girls wearing the uniforms of St. Mary's.

One of the girls glanced at them as she passed. "Hi, Danny!"

Danny was taken aback. "Er . . . Hi, um . . ."

"Judy," Brian whispered.

"Hi, Julie!" Danny said.

The girl gave him a filthy look and hurried a little to catch up with her friends.

Brian thumped Danny on the arm. "You idiot! I said *Judy,* not *Julie!*"

Danny rubbed his arm. "How was *I* to know? I've never even *seen* her before!"

Brian said, "Danny, two weeks ago she spent an hour listening to you going on about how Manchester City were the greatest football team in the world. She was all over you!"

"That was her?"

"How do you do it?" Brian asked. He got up from the wall, pushed back his sleeves and held out his bare arms. "Look at that! I've got muscles! Everyone knows that girls like muscles, but *this* lanky git gets more action than both of us combined!"

Danny said, "Maybe they go for quality over quantity."

Brian sighed, shook his head and sat down again. "So what time's the party tomorrow night, Col?"

"About eight." Like many people, Colin's parents always threw a party for Mystery Day. For Colin's mother, it was really just an excuse for a family get-together. Sometimes Colin felt that his parents only wanted the party so that they could embarrass him in front of his cousins. "You're definitely coming, then?"

"Yeah, but . . . right, here's the thing, OK? My folks are going out and they said it's going to be hard to find a babysitter for Susie. So they asked me to ask you if she could come to your party."

"I'm sure my folks won't mind. And she'll be able to keep my little cousins busy."

"Speak of the devil . . . ," Brian said.

The others looked up to see that Susie was cycling furiously back to them.

"She does *not* look happy," Colin said.

Susie stopped her bike in the middle of the road and glared at them. "Brian!"

"Now what?"

"I'm telling on you!" she yelled across at her brother.

Brian laughed and got to his feet. "OK! OK! I'm coming." He turned back to Colin and Danny. "Right, I'll see you tomorrow. What time did you say the party starts, Col?"

"Eight," Colin said. "You'll be there, right, Danny?"

But Danny wasn't paying attention. He was standing very still and staring into space.

"Danny?"

Suddenly, Danny screamed, "Susie! Get out of the road!"

Colin turned to see the out-of-control bus screeching around the corner. Heading straight for Brian's sister.

Cell 18 was four meters to each side and a little over three meters high. It contained a narrow, uncomfortable bed, a single chair, a small desk, a large, full bookcase, a hand basin and a toilet.

The walls were made of reinforced concrete. There were no windows. The only light came from two small but powerful bulbs set into the ceiling, shielded by unbreakable glass.

A man stood in the center of the room, staring at the blank wall. He had not moved for over an hour.

Later, he would sit on the bed, or perhaps lie on it; he hadn't yet decided. Then again, he might just choose to remain standing.

The wardens referred to him as Joseph.

He was in his early forties. He was tall, thinner now than he had been ten years ago, but by no means skinny, and had long, unkempt black hair and a graying beard.

A decade ago Joseph had been carried, unconscious, into the cell. On his clear days, when he was aware of his situation and his surroundings, Joseph knew that officially he was not a prisoner; there had been no trial and no legal proceedings of any kind. He didn't even know where this cell was located. But the clear days were few; most of the time, Joseph existed only inside his own head, living with his memories and nightmares.

Joseph continued to stare at the wall. Last night he'd had the nightmare again, the same terrifying, recurring dream; visions of blood, pain, murder and death on an overwhelming scale.

Joseph was often glad of his imprisonment. Here, he was safe. No one could harm him. And likewise, he couldn't harm anyone else.

If I'm here, he would say to himself, *then everyone is safe.*

This thought was always followed by a conflicting one: *But I'm not just here, I'm out there too. And if I'm out there, then no one is safe.*

Joseph slowly turned and looked toward the bed. *I could sit. Or I could lie.*

He smiled.

Why not? I've lied before. Sometimes it seems like my whole life has become a lie.

He wondered how long he had been here.

Then he wondered how much time he had left.

How much time the world had left.

2

COLIN UNZIPPED HIS JACKET AND HUNG it in the hall. As he was pulling off his rain-soaked sneakers, he heard his father shouting from the kitchen.

"What time do you call this?"

"It wasn't my fault!" Colin shouted back. He went into the kitchen, where his parents—Warren and Caroline Wagner were sitting at the table.

"It's never your fault," his father said.

"No, really it wasn't."

"Your dinner's in the oven," his mother said. "Another ten minutes and it would have been in the bin. If you're going to be late, the least you could do is let us know."

His father said, "How come your mother leaves the school at the same time that you do and she's always home hours before you are? Maybe the teachers have access to a special shortcut that the students don't know about—is that it?"

"But it *wasn't* my fault!" Colin said. "Let me tell you what happened." He sat down at the table and looked at his parents.

They looked back at him and he could see from their expressions that they were both thinking, *This had better be good.*

"OK, well . . . Me and Brian and Danny were hanging around at the corner of the park . . ."

His mother interrupted him. "What were you up to?"

"Nothing. We were just talking. Anyway, Susie came up on her bike to tell Brian that he had to go home and then . . ." Colin paused. "I don't really know *exactly* what happened—someone said that there was a fight on the bus and the driver turned around to look—but anyway, the thing is, Susie's there in the middle of the road and all of a sudden the bus comes screeching around the corner. Heading right for her. And the next thing we know there's this really loud *crunch* as the bus hits her bike."

Caroline Wagner put her hands to her mouth. "Oh my God!"

"No, no!" Colin said. "Mum, she's OK, she's fine! I don't know how he did it, but Danny saved her! He ran across, picked her up and saved her life! It was brilliant! She went all white and she was shaking and everything, but apart from that she was OK. Her bike was wrecked, though. And she wouldn't let go of Danny for ages. Now she'll be even more nuts about him. The police came and an ambulance and everything, but they didn't need it. No one was really hurt."

"You're sure she was OK?"

Colin nodded. "She was. It only took her a few minutes to start blaming Brian for the accident, so that means she was back to normal."

"Who were the ambulance crew?" his father asked. He was a paramedic, based at the local hospital.

"I didn't recognize them." Around a mouthful of mashed potato and peas, he added, "but they checked her over and said she was OK."

Colin's mother gave him her famous thin-lipped look, the one that told him she *wanted* to believe him, but wasn't so sure. "You promise you're not making this up?"

"No, it really happened!" Colin waved his cutlery around, demonstrating: "The bus came *brrrrrmm* around the corner, really fast, and Susie was here, OK? And we were on the corner and all of a sudden Danny was like . . . *zoom*! One second he was right next to me and the next he'd scooped Susie up in his arms and was lying on the far side of the road, holding on to her. Then the bus went *screeee* because the driver hit the brakes, but it was too late because he still hit the bike."

Colin's parents looked at each other. His dad said, very quietly, "I see."

"It's true," Colin said. "I swear! You can ask Danny or Brian."

"That was . . . very brave of Danny," his mother said, "and very stupid of Susie to just stop in the middle of the road."

"Yeah, I know. You should have seen Brian's face, though. I thought he was going to throw up or faint or something."

Mr. Wagner pushed himself back from the table and got to his feet. "I'd better phone Susie's parents, see if they need anything. And Danny's parents too."

"He's fine," Colin said. "There wasn't a scratch on him."

"Well, I'll phone them anyway. Danny might have gone into shock." He went out into the hall, closing the door behind him.

"So," Colin's mother said, "will Danny be coming to the party tomorrow?"

Colin nodded. "Yeah, I think so. And Brian says his parents are going out and they wanted to know if Susie could come too. So I said it was OK. Who else is coming?"

His mother began to list the friends and relatives who had been invited to the party. There were the usual last-minute cancellations and changes, and Colin found himself wondering why they couldn't go to someone else's.

"And I don't want you staying up late tonight. We're going to have a full day tomorrow getting everything ready."

"But I want to see Max Dalton's interview!"

"You can tape it and watch it in the morning."

"You just said that we're going to have a full day tomorrow!"

"Then you can watch it the day after."

"Then I'll be the only one who hasn't seen it!"

Caroline Wagner sighed. "All right, then. You can stay up for it. Now finish your dinner."

After dinner, Colin phoned Brian. "So are you coming out tonight?"

"Are you *kidding*?" Brian said. "My folks went mad about what nearly happened to Susie! They said it was my fault for teasing her. I added up all their punishments and apparently I'm grounded until I'm sixty-one. They're not even letting me go to your party tomorrow night!"

"You could tell them that you have to come so that you can thank Danny for saving Susie's life."

"I already thought of that, but they told me to phone him instead. You know what Susie did? Remember when I had my camera last summer? Well, she took all my photos that Danny was in and she put them up all over her bedroom wall."

Colin laughed.

"Mad, isn't it? And you know something else? You know the way we have to write about one of the heroes for homework? Well, Susie's class has to write an essay called 'My Hero,' and she's going to write about Danny." He let out a long sigh. "God, he's going to have even more girls after him now! And it's not as though he's *really* a hero. I mean, he just happened to have been looking in the right direction to see the bus. Any one of us could have done it."

"There was no way he could have seen the bus coming from where we were standing. He must have heard it." Colin paused. "Though I've always had good hearing and *I* didn't hear it coming. Did you?"

"No."

"Then how did he know?"

Brian didn't have an answer for that one.

"And how *did* he move so fast?" Colin asked. "I mean, one second he was right next to me, the next he was picking Susie up."

"I suppose . . . Col, I wasn't looking in the right direction. I heard Danny shouting at her, so I turned to look at him. I mean, I was looking right at Susie. I turned to look at Danny when he shouted, but he was gone. And then I looked back and they were on the ground on the other side of the road. I didn't actually *see* it happen. Did you?"

"I did," Colin said. "He was just a blur."

"But my point is this: he did it in the time it took me to turn my head twice." They both fell silent again, then, slowly and carefully, Brian said, "Col, that's not possible. No one can move that fast."

"Not these days, anyway," Colin said. "Not since all the superhumans disappeared."

There was another long pause.

Brian said, "What if . . . ?" He stopped. "Nah, that's crazy."

"What?"

"Well, what if *Danny* is a superhuman?"

Most of the prison was underground. From the air, it looked like a small, isolated farmhouse. Its exact location was known only to a small handful of people. Even the prison doctor didn't know how to find the place on his own; he was driven to and from the prison in a truck with blacked-out windows.

Warden Mills stood in the doorway, squinting his eyes to shield them from the dust stirred up by the twin rotors of the descending Boeing CH-47 Chinook helicopter. Even before the copter touched down, the rear ramp was dropped and fourteen people disembarked. The woman was dressed in a simple black trouser suit with a white blouse and flat shoes, but the thirteen men were wearing crisp army fatigues and all were heavily armed.

"What's all this?" the warden asked.

"Random inspection," the woman said.

"But we just had one last month!"

"I think you'll find that the key word is 'random.' It wouldn't be a random inspection if you knew we were coming, would it?"

"Guess not."

Mills led them along the hall and down into the storm cellar, where a hidden door slid back to reveal the wide stone stairway that led into the prison.

As the men began to unpack their equipment, Mills turned to the woman. "How long will this take?"

"Not long," she said. "Anything to report?"

"No." That annoyed the warden a little; they were aware of everything that happened—they even monitored *his* vital signs—but they still felt they had to ask him stupid questions.

One of the men sat down at the warden's computer and began tapping away at the keyboard. The other men took out sophisticated scanning devices and started to check the integrity of the doors and walls. Two men made several trips back up to the helicopter, bringing in heavier equipment.

"So," Mills said to the woman. "How's life in the outside world? It's Mystery Day, right?"

"You know I'm not allowed to discuss such things with you."

"I kind of miss the celebrations."

The woman didn't respond to that. Instead, she examined her clipboard. "Now . . . I've been ordered to check on the prisoners."

Another test, the warden said to himself. "Not possible. No one but me and Doc McLean get to see the prisoners. You know that."

"We'll need your access codes to override the locks," the woman said.

"Yes, you would. *If* you were getting to see the prisoners. Which you're not."

"I'm not asking you, Warden Mills. I'm telling you. Give us the codes."

"You know I can't do that without a signed order from Central Command," Mills said with a smile, to give the impression that he was playing along. Inwardly, he was beginning to get worried. They occasionally sprung surprises on him, but this one felt wrong.

The woman turned to one of the soldiers. "Davison?"

The soldier stepped up to Warden Mills, saluted and said, "Sir! Direct order from Central Command, sir! You are to provide us with the override codes necessary for us to access the cells, sir!"

"I'm afraid I can't do that, soldier."

The warden found himself facing the dangerous end of a gun. He sighed. "Son, put the gun away. You're embarrassing yourself." He turned to the woman. "Now, I know that you've been ordered to put me to the test, but let's not, and say we did, OK?"

The soldier fired.

Mills glanced down to see a tranquilizer dart protruding from his chest. He collapsed to the floor.

Davison leaned down and smiled at him. "We know you've got a biometric implant that will trigger an alarm if your vital signs fluctuate, Warden Mills. Can't have that happening." He reached out and pulled down on the warden's eyelids, closing them. "Don't worry, you're not dying. I'm just closing your eyes to prevent them from drying up. You've been dosed with a muscle relaxant. You'll be paralyzed for about seven hours."

"We have to move fast," the woman said. "Get those doors open!"

One of the technicians said, "We won't have time to open them all."

The woman said, "We don't *need* to open them all. Just . . ." She checked one of the computer screens. "Just Cell 18. The man we're looking for is called Joseph."

3

LATER, AS HE WAS ATTEMPTING TO DO his homework, Colin couldn't get the thought out of his mind: *Suppose it's true? Suppose Danny is a superhuman? Maybe he's been one all along, but kept it secret. Or maybe Danny didn't even know. This could be the first time he's ever done anything like that.*

If superpowers are inherited, wouldn't that mean that one of Danny's parents is a superhuman too?

Colin dismissed this idea almost immediately; Danny's parents were just too ordinary. Danny's father was a manager in the local supermarket and his mother was a driving instructor. Danny also had a seven-year-old brother, Niall. If Danny had inherited superhuman powers from one of his parents, then that would mean that Niall might also become a superhuman.

Colin forced himself to focus on his homework. A single four-page essay. That shouldn't take more than a couple of hours; then he would be completely free of homework worry for the rest of the weekend.

He was lying on his bed, on his stomach, with his homework book open on the floor at the foot of the bed. He had half a page done and he wasn't happy with it. He'd been trying Brian's idea of writing from the point of view of one of the villains, but it was proving to be tougher than he'd expected.

OK. Concentrate! Suppose I had superhuman powers . . . Say I could fly. That'd be cool!

While he was daydreaming about joining the school's athletics team—if he could fly, he'd be a champion long jumper—a thought came into his mind: *I wonder if* Danny *will be able to fly?*

Maybe Danny won't want his powers and he'll find a way to give them to me.

Colin sighed and looked down at his homework again.

"I'm not getting anywhere with this," he muttered to himself. *OK. Start over.*

He turned to a blank page and began to write: "If I was a superhero, I wouldn't even tell my best friends because that would put them in danger. I would have to come up with some good excuses for always disappearing to go off and save people."

Danny's never done that, so maybe he's not a superhuman after all. But then, how did *he do it? How did he move fast enough to rescue Susie?*

Colin looked at the few lines he'd written, put his homework book away and wandered downstairs to the sitting room.

"How's the essay coming along?" Colin's dad asked.

Colin sat down on the floor with his back to the television set. The sound was off and clearly his parents hadn't been watching it. "Not great. I don't really know all *that* much about superhumans. What was it like when they were around? It must have been strange."

His father said, "I was about your age when the first superhumans began to appear. You know the way they always keep weird stories until the end of the news? Well, that's what it was like, for a while. It was all, 'And finally, it seems that in New York there's a new force fighting evil.' That kind of thing."

"But weren't people scared?"

"No, because for a long time most people didn't *really* believe it. Not until Paragon went up against Façade."

"Why? Why was that any different?"

"Because everyone saw it happening live on television. It was in Detroit, one of those charity telethon events, like Comic Relief. They were trying to raise twenty million dollars for . . . can't remember what it was now."

"Education," Colin's mother said.

"Right, education. Anyway, it's all just about over, and they're going on about how much money they've raised, then all of a sudden one of the guest musicians comes out and he just transforms himself into Façade. He's got a whole bunch of thugs with him and Façade demands fifty million dollars or the studio audience and all these celebrities will be killed. Façade is strutting about, showing off his powers by shape-shifting into different people, when Paragon just drops out of the ceiling and lands on top of him. *Bam!* One punch to the head and Façade is out cold! A couple of his henchmen turn their guns on Paragon, but he just flies right into them, knocking them over. Then he launched a dozen gas grenades. The gas instantly sent everyone in the studio—even the hostages—to sleep. The cameras were still running, though, so we could watch him tying up Façade and his men."

"It would have been a great court case too," Caroline said, "if Façade hadn't escaped from custody on the way to the trial."

"What about Paragon, though? If he arrived so quickly, doesn't that suggest that he lived nearby? I mean, from what I've read about him he wasn't able to fly very fast."

"Maybe he just happened to be close by for some other reason," Caroline said.

"Yeah, but . . . I suppose the police had the TV studio surrounded, right? That means that Paragon would have had to get past them in order to get into the studio. So you know what I'm thinking?"

"What's that?" his father asked.

"Maybe Paragon was a cop. In his real life, I mean. Maybe they knew all about him."

"I doubt it, Colin. Even if he was, he wouldn't have let anyone know that he was Paragon. The only heroes whose real names we knew were the Daltons. And that was only because they were already rich enough to protect themselves. All the others probably had ordinary lives." Warren looked up at the television set. "Speaking of which . . . Only a few minutes to go before Max Dalton's interview. Right, Colin—put the kettle on."

"It's not my turn!"

"It is if you want to stay up and find out what Max Dalton has to say for himself."

As Colin carried the mugs of tea into the sitting room, the specially extended edition of the ten o'clock news was coming to an end. It had already reported that Times Square in Manhattan was blocked with people. The news report showed a sea of banners and flags, cheering people dressed up as their favorite heroes and mounted policemen attempting to keep the crowds under control.

The TV cut back to the female newsreader. "And after tonight's exclusive interview with Max Dalton, we'll be opening tomorrow's poll: 'If you had to be a superhuman, which one would you be?' You can choose between Titan, Apex, Paragon or Max Dalton. We'll have the results this time tomorrow night, with updates throughout the day."

The male newsreader chuckled. "Thanks, Diana. No Ragnarök on the list, then?"

"Oh, I don't think *he'd* get too many votes, Tom, do you?"

"Guess not! You can vote by pressing the red button on your remote, through the website or by phone. Calls cost . . ."

Colin's father hit the mute button, then said, "So who would *you* choose, Colin?"

"I don't know," Colin said. "Sometimes I'd like to be Thalamus, because he was the smartest man on the planet. But I kind of like Joshua Dalton too."

Colin's mother asked, "Because he was rich and he's had a string of supermodel girlfriends?"

"Mostly because he has his own helicopter. I'd love to have a go in a helicopter." Colin turned around to look at his father. "So why do you think that only The High Command survived?"

"Maybe they *all* survived, Colin. Did you ever think of that? Maybe they all survived and decided that it was time to retire."

Colin laughed. "Oh yeah, sure. If you had the sort of power that Titan had, you'd never be able to just sit around when some disaster happened. You'd have to try and help. That's what Titan was like."

"You don't think that he could have just decided that he'd done enough?"

"No. I mean, *I* wouldn't. Titan was the most powerful man

ever. He had a responsibility to use his powers to help everyone else."

All this talk about superheroes reminded Colin of his earlier conversation with Brian.

"Dad . . . Remember what I was saying about how Danny saved Susie's life?"

"Yes . . . ," his father said cautiously.

"Well, me and Brian were thinking about it. Danny was really, really fast. Maybe he's a superhuman."

"How? How could he be? Apart from the Daltons, there aren't any superhumans left anymore."

"But the way Danny moved . . ." Colin shook his head. "I saw it myself and I still can't believe it."

"The mind can play tricks on you, Colin," said his mother. "Especially under a stressful situation. It might just have *seemed* a lot faster than it was."

"I suppose . . . But, you see, I was thinking about this, right? Most of the superheroes got their powers when they were teenagers and Danny's about the right age."

Warren grinned. "Are you seriously suggesting that your friend Danny Cooper has hidden powers?"

"Well, it seems like it."

"Then let us know if he learns how to fly. That could come in handy."

Colin's mother said, "It's starting!"

Colin pulled one of the cushions off the sofa and stretched out on the floor, facing the television set.

The screen showed lots of old footage of the superheroes in action—most of it very shaky and out of focus—then cut to a black-and-white photograph of a handsome gray-haired man in his midforties.

"Maxwell Edwin Dalton," the presenter's voice said. "Billionaire CEO of MaxEdDal Pharmaceuticals, first came to public notice when . . ."

Colin twisted around to face his mother. "What's CEO mean?"

"Chief executive officer," she replied. "The boss, in other words."

Colin turned back to see that the screen was now showing the outside of the MaxEdDal headquarters in Manhattan. "At the age of fifteen," the voice continued, "young Max Dalton discovered that he had the ability to know what other people were thinking, and to some degree influence their thoughts to make them do what he wanted. Yet, unlike most other superhumans, he chose to go public with his abilities. With his younger sister and brother, Roz and Joshua, he formed The High Command." The screen showed photos of the Daltons as teenagers.

"Is that the best they can do?" Colin asked. "Isn't there any film of Max in action? You know, actually *doing* something?"

It was another fifteen minutes before the presenter finally said, "Tonight, Maxwell Dalton will give his first interview since the events of the original Mystery Day. That's next, coming right up after this!"

The television cut to a commercial. Colin yawned.

"I heard that the TV stations are charging a fortune for these ads," Caroline said. "Twice as much as they charge for ads during the Super Bowl."

When the program finally returned, the interviewer was sitting behind a desk. To his right, on a long leather sofa, sat Max Dalton. He was dressed in a sports jacket, white shirt open at the collar and faded jeans.

"He looks, well, kind of ordinary," Colin said. "I thought he'd be bigger."

"Shhh!"

"Thank you for joining us, Mr. Dalton," the interviewer said.

"It's my pleasure, Garth," Dalton said, smiling. His teeth were the whitest Colin had ever seen.

"Now, first, I guess the most obvious question—and one that I'm sure most people want to know—is why now? Why, after all these years, have you decided to finally break your silence?"

Max paused for a second. "Tomorrow's the tenth anniversary. I think ten years is long enough to wait."

"Tell me this, Max . . . Can you read my mind right now?"

Smiling, Max said, "Garth, I don't do that sort of thing anymore. Those days are gone."

"Tell us about those days, if you will."

"Much of what has been written about my life as a superhero is apocryphal at best."

"Apocryphal?" Colin asked.

"Made-up," his mother said.

Max continued. "Yes, we fought crime, helped people, tried to make the world a better place. If you've been given a gift—like I was—you're honor-bound to use it for the greater good."

"And can you tell us what happened ten years ago?"

"Despite what a lot of people have been saying, I wasn't there. So your guess is as good as mine, Garth. All I know is that Ragnarök had built some enormous machine and was driving it straight for Manhattan. Then . . . Well, who can say? There was a big explosion and that was it. No more superhumans."

"Except yourself—and your brother and sister."

Max nodded. "Exactly. I have no idea what happened. Josh and I visited the site the following day. All we found was a lot of wreckage."

"No bodies?"

"No."

"Doesn't that seem strange, that you have no more of an idea what happened than we do? Surely you must know *something*!"

"Now, that's why I don't usually do interviews. You have to remember that we lost some very good friends during that battle. Energy, Quantum, Titan, Apex, Paragon . . . all the others. We fought alongside them for *years*."

"I know, but—"

Max interrupted him. "Do you think that if I knew something I'd just sit back and let it go? Would you? If some of your closest friends suddenly disappeared, wouldn't you want to investigate it? We did everything we could to find out what had happened to them."

The interviewer said, "Can you tell me, then, why you and the other members of The High Command weren't present at that final battle?"

"We might have been superheroes," Max said, "but even *we* couldn't be in two places at one time."

"But there were other superhumans who *weren't* present, and they've also disappeared."

"This is apparently true," Max said.

"Care to suggest how that might be?"

"No," Max said. "I mean, I've got a few ideas, but nothing concrete. Nothing that hasn't been suggested before. Maybe they retired from the business, just as I did."

"And may I ask, why *did* you retire? If you don't mind speaking about that."

"Whatever happened ten years ago . . . Well, as I said, your guess is as good as mine. We do know that every other superhuman in the world disappeared that day, heroes and villains included. Roz, Josh and I talked about it—at length—and we came to the conclusion that with all the supervillains gone, we weren't needed anymore."

"Yes, but—"

Max interrupted him. "We realized that we could do more good by focusing our efforts on other areas of our lives. MaxEdDal Pharmaceuticals specializes in effective, low-cost medicines that have certainly saved more lives than I ever could have as a superhero."

"Don't you miss those days?"

"At times . . . but I don't miss the constant struggles, or the fear that one day a new supervillain might emerge who would be powerful enough to destroy the planet. At least we know that if there are no more superhumans, there will be no more supervillains."

Max Dalton turned to look directly into the camera. "So for better or worse—and I firmly believe that it's for the better—the age of the superhumans is over."

4

VICTOR CROSS SAT IN A DARK ROOM, THE
only light coming from the two computer screens in front of him.

His fingers flew over the keyboard as, on one screen, computer code appeared line after line, page after page.

On the second screen, a complex computer-generated image of a large silver ball rotated slowly. Cross watched this as he typed. He didn't need to watch the other screen. He knew exactly what was on it.

The letters and symbols on his keyboard had been worn away on all but two of the keys: backspace and delete. Victor very rarely used them. He didn't make mistakes.

Cross was twenty years old, tall with an athletic build. He normally kept his blond hair short, but it had been months since he'd last had time to get it cut, and it now hung over his face.

The phone beside him buzzed once. Victor hit the "Speaker" button. "Talk to me."

"It's me. What's the situation?" The voice was electronically disguised, giving it an artificial, machinelike quality.

"I've just heard from the extraction team. They've got Joseph."

"Good. You know what you have to do?"

"Of course. We're all prepped and ready."

"The tech team are on their way to you now. They should be there within the hour."

"Good," Victor said. "My own team are going to be working

around the clock on the nucleus. It'll take a couple of days. You're sure that we can contain him for that long?"

"Shouldn't be a problem. Keep me posted." The call was disconnected.

Victor continued typing at the same ferocious speed.

He had a complete mental image of the computer program he was writing. All his fingers were doing was transferring the program from his brain into the computer.

Even as he typed, his mind was occupied with several other matters. In the background, he was considering ways to speed up the typing process. The ideal solution would be some sort of human-machine interface through which he could upload his programs directly into the computer. That would save a tremendous amount of time.

At the same time, he was wondering how to deal with the coming situation. He knew from experience that not everything would go according to plan, because other people were involved. Computers did what you told them to do, but people had a tendency to do what they *believed* they were supposed to do.

He set another part of his brain working on ideas for alternative plans, just in case anything went wrong.

Victor was aware that most people didn't—or couldn't—use their brains in the way that he used his. The average person could keep no more than six or seven different thoughts going at once, and most of those were of the "what will I have for dinner?" variety.

But Victor could run dozens of different thought processes at the same time; he could program his brain as efficiently as he could program a computer.

A mental alarm reminded him that he'd now been working for eight solid hours and that it was time to take a break.

Victor pushed himself back from the computer terminal, yawned and ran his hands through his hair.

The phone buzzed again. "Mr. Cross?"

"What do you want, Jeff?"

"Can you spare a few minutes?"

"What's the problem?"

"We're having trouble getting the nucleus up to speed. Or, rather, we *can* get it up to speed, but then it's not stable."

"Sounds like an imbalance in the mag-lev platform. Put Rose on to it. She's the expert."

"I already asked her, Mr. Cross. She said you told her the diagnostic scanner was more important than anything else."

"All right. I'll talk to her."

Victor Cross left his office, went out onto the walkway and peered down at the cavern below. Dozens of people—most of them in military uniforms—milled about.

In all, the complex was currently home to over a hundred people, with another hundred expected to arrive within the next day.

As Victor walked along the rough-hewn corridors, he met two workers awkwardly carrying a life-sized glass statue of a girl. Victor stopped them. "I told you to bring her to the upper storeroom. That's up on level one. She already *was* on level one! What are you doing down here with her?"

The two men exchanged a nervous glance. One of them said, "Er . . . It kind of fell. Over the rail."

Victor glared at them. *"What?"*

"It was an accident, sir! I tripped and, well, it just fell over the edge. I tried to grab it but it slipped out of my hands." The man nodded to his companion and they set the statue back on its feet.

Victor walked around it, examining it carefully. It appeared to be intact, other than the finger marks in the light coating of dust.

"She fell from level one down to here? That's six floors. And no fractures, cracks or chips. Not even a scratch."

"Yes, sir. Sorry. I don't know what this thing is made out of, Mr. Cross, but it's not glass. Whatever it is, it seems to be absolutely invulnerable."

5

passed off the same as it had every year; the adults all drank too much and started singing, and the younger kids fought over board games.

After a couple of hours, Colin and Danny decided that going for a walk was a more attractive option than listening to Colin's uncle Norman trying to entertain everyone by repeating the same old jokes he'd told the previous year.

Colin and Danny walked in silence for a couple of minutes, shoulders hunched against the rain, until Colin was sure that there was no one around.

"So . . . How did you do it, Dan?"

"How did I do what?"

"You know what I'm talking about. How did you move fast enough to save Susie?"

Danny shrugged. "Just lucky, I suppose."

"That wasn't luck."

"Of course it was. What else could it be?"

"That's what I've been wondering about all day. The speed that bus came around the corner . . . I went back there this afternoon, just to have a look. There's no way any normal person could have run that fast."

"Well, obviously *I* did."

"But you're not a normal person, are you, Dan? You're a superhuman."

Danny laughed. "Are you nuts?"

"You lucky—! I'd give *anything* to be a superhuman!"

"I'm not a superhuman!"

"OK, OK," Colin said. After a few seconds, he said, "So, was that the first time?"

"The first time what?"

"You *know* what I'm asking. Has anything like that ever happened before?"

"No. Of course not. It was a fluke."

"What did your parents say?"

"Ah, you know the way parents are. My mother kept focusing on the wrong things. Like asking what Susie was doing in the middle of the road and why I hadn't just come straight home from school—that sort of thing."

"What about your dad?"

"He just said, 'Well done!'"

"That's it? You saved a little girl's life and he just said, 'Well done!'?"

"What *else* would he say?"

Colin carefully considered his response. "He could have asked you what *I* asked you. If you were a superhuman."

Danny paused. "Well, he didn't ask me that."

"*I'm* asking."

"I know."

"And?"

"And I keep telling you! I'm not a superhuman, OK? Just leave it!" Danny walked away. "I'm going home. Thanks for the party."

Colin hesitated for a second, then went after him. "Wait, wait!"

Without turning around or slowing down, Danny said, "What?"

"Just tell me the truth. Please. I swear I won't say anything to anyone else! I just have to know. If you don't tell me, then I'm going to be wondering about it for the rest of my life."

"There's nothing to tell."

"Nothing to tell *me*. I'm supposed to be your best friend!"

Danny stopped walking. His shoulders sagged.

"Swear that you won't tell anyone?"

"I swear."

"Especially not Brian, OK?"

"I promise!"

Danny took a deep breath and looked away. "It started happening a couple of months ago. Like, I'd be listening to a song on the radio and all of a sudden it would slow way down, like it was being played at the wrong speed. I went out on my bike on Saturday morning and cycled all the way around the park. It usually takes me a quarter of an hour, right? I did it in under five minutes. But it didn't *feel* like I was moving any faster, more like everything else had slowed down. Things . . . things are changing. Inside me." Danny swallowed. "It's . . . it's kind of freaking me out a bit. It's like I've got no control over it. I mean, I could run home now and be there before you can blink. Or it might not work at all."

The two friends stared at each other.

"So it's true," Colin said. "You're a superhuman."

"It's looking like that." A smile slowly grew on Danny's face. "I really shouldn't have told you."

"God, you are so lucky! You know what I'd do if I was you? I'd join the athletics team. I'd win first place every time! It would be great!"

Danny shook his head. "Nah."

"Seriously," Colin said. "You should do it. You could be the next . . ." He paused. "Who's a good runner?"

"I'd rather be a soccer player."

"You could do that, then! You could try out for Man United! They'd snap you up in a second!"

Danny grinned. "Or I could even try out for one of the *good* teams."

"So, show me! Do something!"

"It might not work."

"Give it a go anyway."

Danny looked up and down the street. There was no one around. "Watch this!" He reached down to the ground and picked up a small white stone. He handed it to Colin. "You'll recognize that stone again, right?"

Colin turned it over in his hands. "Sure. I suppose."

"Now throw it."

"Where?"

"Down the road."

"OK." Colin reached back his arm and flung the stone into the darkness. He didn't see where it landed, but assumed that it must have hit a patch of grass, because it made no sound.

He turned back to Danny. "So?"

Danny smiled, held up his hand and opened it. The stone was resting in his palm.

"How . . . ?"

"I caught it," Danny said.

"But you didn't even move!"

"Yes, I did. I ran after the stone and picked it out of the air."

Colin laughed. "That's amazing!"

Danny frowned. "Now the power's just gone again. I suppose that I'll be able to turn it on and off at will eventually. In the meantime, I have to be careful—and you'd better not say anything to anyone!"

"I won't, I won't . . . So you're going to be a superhero! God, I wish it was me! How does it feel?"

"Weird, I suppose. It's like I *exist* faster. When I'm doing it, I don't really feel I'm running that fast. It's more like everything else around me has slowed way down, like the rest of the world has gone into slow motion. And the more I concentrate on it, the slower everything becomes."

"Are you going to tell your parents?"

"Actually . . . That's the really strange thing about all this." He hesitated. "All right, I know I can trust you. The strange thing is that *they* told *me,* in a way. Once they heard what happened with Susie, Dad told me everything. He said that he was sure I'd figure it out anyway. And he's teaching me to control the power too. He said that you have to focus on it, kind of like meditation. You let yourself relax, clear your mind of everything except the power. I wasn't able to do it, though. He said that it takes a while to learn."

"How does he know all this?"

"You swear that you won't tell anyone?"

"I swear."

"Sometimes—though not always—it's hereditary. Dad was a superhuman too."

Colin's mouth dropped open. *"You're serious?"*

"Yeah."

"Someone famous?"

"Believe it or not, my father used to be Quantum."

6

JOSEPH STEPPED DOWN FROM THE HELI-
copter and looked around. He was wearing a pair of sunglasses
one of the soldiers had given him, but the light from the setting
sun still hurt his eyes.

The copter had landed at the bottom of a small canyon,
barely a hundred meters across. A set of huge steel doors was set
into the canyon wall.

"Who are you?" he asked the woman. "What is this place?"

"Call me Rachel. We're in California. It's an abandoned
gold mine."

"How long was I locked up?"

"Ten years. Almost to the day. I have to know . . . your abilities?"

He gave her a weak smile. "Gone, of course. Do you think
I'd have stayed there if I'd still had my powers? It was only a concrete cell. Why . . . Why did you wait so long?"

"After the battle-tank, everything fell apart. It's taken us this
long to rebuild. It's not as though we could operate openly. And
no one knew where you were."

They began to walk toward the steel doors, which were now
slowly creaking open.

A young man walked out and stopped in front of them.
"Joseph, I presume?"

Joseph nodded. "Who are you?"

"This is Victor Cross," Rachel said. "He's the one who tracked you down."

Cross said, "We have some quarters set up for you. They should be a lot more pleasant than your prison cell."

"You know who I am?"

"Of course. I know everything about you."

Joseph stood in silence for a few seconds, then said, "I know I'm not the man I once was, Mr. Cross, and I'm very much afraid that all that time as a prisoner has affected me. I find it hard to focus and even the smallest of things can distract me, but I'm not *entirely* stupid. Why did you wait so long before freeing me?"

Victor regarded him for a moment. "Honestly?"

"Yes. Honestly."

"We didn't need you until now."

"I see. I feel . . . different. Clearer. Were they doing something to me in that place? Drugging me—to keep me docile?"

"Almost certainly," Victor said.

"And what about the boy? What's happening there?"

Victor ignored the question and called over two workers. "Escort this gentleman to the med-lab. We'll be there shortly. Give him anything he wants, understood?"

Joseph smiled. "How old are you, Cross?"

"Almost twenty-one."

"So you're too young to have been one of us, then? You weren't a superhuman?"

"No. I was only ten years old when Ragnarök's machine was used."

Joseph smiled again and nodded.

Rachel and Victor watched as he was led away.

"What do you think?" Victor asked.

She shrugged. "He was definitely being drugged back at the prison. Some sort of low-level scopolamine to keep him relaxed and compliant. It should be completely out of his system in the next couple of hours."

"It had better *not* be," Victor said. "We *want* him relaxed and compliant. Make sure he stays that way, got it?"

"Sure."

She followed Victor into the mine.

"So . . . the breakout was a success," Rachel said.

"Obviously."

"I'll write up a full report for you."

Without looking at her, Victor said, "We have Joseph and you weren't traced. What's to report?"

"We left the warden alive, but it'll be a few more hours before he wakes."

Victor nodded.

Rachel followed him up the metal stairway. "Don't you want to know who the other inmates were?"

"Not really."

"You did a good job locating the prison."

Victor stopped outside his office and turned to her. "Rachel, I have work to do. If you want to make small talk, find some-one else."

He went into his office and closed the door behind him. He sat down at his desk, switched on his computer and keyed a number into his phone.

The call was answered immediately. It was the electronically disguised voice again.

"Talk to me," the voice said.

"We have him," Victor said.

"Good," the voice said. "You're at your terminal?"

"Yes."

"Find the file called *Protégé*. The password is 'Apotheosis.' The file will tell you everything you need to know. Got that?"

"Got it." Victor disconnected the call and began typing.

He found the file, entered the password and read through it.

Then he made another phone call. After a couple of seconds, a man's voice said, "Hello?"

Reading from the computer screen, Victor said, "Icebreaker."

There was a pause. "Say again?"

"Icebreaker."

Another pause and the man sighed. Then he said, "Damocles."

Victor read the countercode. "Ultimatum."

The man said, "I . . . I understand." After a brief discussion, he gave Victor his location, then asked, "When?"

"Within the hour. Be ready. This is a *code-one* extraction. Do you understand what that means?"

"Yes. It means that you want the boys no matter what it takes. Everything else is secondary. All lives are expendable. Even my own."

7

DANNY COOPER'S FATHER WAS IN THE sitting room watching television when Danny arrived home. "You're late."

"Sorry," Danny said. "The party went on longer than I expected."

"All right. Good party, was it?"

"It was OK. Everyone kept asking me about what happened with Susie."

"You didn't tell any of your friends, did you?"

"No, of course not!" Danny lied.

Danny's father hesitated for a second, then nodded. "Good, good. Actually, Dan, if you're not too tired, I think you and I need to have a little talk. I need to show you something important." He pushed his massive frame out of his armchair and stretched.

"At this hour?"

Mr. Cooper turned off the television set. "It won't take long." He led Danny out into the hall.

"Keep the noise down," he whispered. "Your mother and Niall are asleep. Now, look at this . . ."

Danny watched as his father pulled the casing off the fuse box in the hall.

"There's a switch . . ." Danny's father groped around and there was a soft *click*.

He turned to the large photo of Danny's grandfather that

hung in the hall and lifted it off its hook. Danny saw that there was a panel behind it. Danny's father pulled the panel open and removed a small black canvas bag.

"What's that?"

"Just some stuff from the old days." He closed the panel and re-hung the photo. He slung the bag over his shoulder and opened the front door.

"Aw, Dad! I don't want to go back out into the rain *again*!"

"It won't hurt you," Danny's father said.

They left the blocks of flats and walked in the direction of the main road. "What's up?" Danny asked.

His father opened the bag and took out a small metal device, about the size of a personal stereo. He flipped a switch on the device and a small red light began blinking.

"What's that for?" Danny asked.

"It's a transponder," his father explained. "I'm sure that these days they could make something like this about the size of your fingernail, but it was state of the art back then."

"I thought that transponders were something to do with aircraft."

"Not necessarily. It's looking for a specific signal. When it gets it, it sends a countersignal back. Someone with the right equipment will be able to pick up our signal and find us. Doesn't matter where we are on the planet, they'll find us."

"Who?"

"You'll see soon enough."

Danny considered this. "So . . . this is a mission, then?"

"Yeah, sort of."

Danny grinned. "Cool! But what if someone recognizes me? Shouldn't I have a mask?"

"It's not really *that* kind of mission, Danny."

"We should have left a note for Mum. I mean, just in case anything happens."

"No, better if she doesn't know. I didn't tell her everything that I did when I was Quantum. Can't have her worried all the time."

"Do you still have your old costume?"

Mr. Cooper smiled. "It wouldn't fit you. Not yet, anyway. You'll need to fill out a bit."

Danny realized that they were heading in the direction of Colin's house and suddenly felt worried. He shouldn't have told Colin about his powers. *What if we* are *going to Colin's?* he wondered. *Suppose Colin says something, lets it slip that he knows?*

For a second, Danny wondered if he could race ahead to Colin's house, tell him not to say a word, then run back without his dad noticing that he'd gone.

No. That wouldn't work. Anyway, we can't be going to Colin's house. Why would we?

Despite the fact that he hadn't got out of bed until midday, Colin was exhausted. He felt dizzy, almost nauseated, as he removed his clothes and dropped them on the floor.

Danny's a superhuman.

The thought jumped into his mind, as it seemed to do every couple of minutes.

He turned off the light, pulled back the blankets and awkwardly climbed into bed; the muscles in his arms and legs were sore, as though he'd been working out all day. This had been happening on and off for weeks now; growing pains, his mother called them.

Danny's going to be off saving the world and having fantastic adventures, while the rest of us have ordinary, boring lives. It's not fair. I want to have superpowers! I want to be able to move as fast as Quantum!

Colin knew that he'd never be able to sleep with these thoughts running around in his head.

He rolled over onto his side and tried to think of something—anything—to keep his mind off the fact that his best friend was going to be a superhero.

It wasn't working.

Colin shifted around to his favorite position—on his back, with his hands tucked behind his head—and tried to focus on the gentle hum of the traffic on the motorway; this usually helped him drift off to sleep.

But this time, as he focused on the noise of the traffic, it seemed to him that the sounds were becoming sharper.

Outside, on the next street, a car beeped its horn twice.

Someone saying good-bye. His own aunt had done the same thing earlier. *Why* do *people do that? Surely getting into the car and driving away is a pretty good indication that you're leaving. You don't have to beep your horn and wake the whole neighborhood up!*

He wondered who it was and listened carefully. He faintly heard a woman calling, "Bye!" as the car pulled away. Colin recognized her voice: Mrs. Healy from number 23. He heard her close her front door, then go into her kitchen and fill the kettle.

I'm dreaming, Colin thought. *There's no way I can hear Mrs. Healy filling her kettle!*

He imagined that he could hear his parents downstairs in the sitting room. The television was on, but they weren't paying attention to it. His father was about to fall asleep; Colin could hear his breathing slowing, becoming more regular. His mother was humming quietly to herself and . . . yes, she was reading; Colin could hear the pages turning.

Colin sat up. A thin film of cold sweat had broken out on the back of his neck and he felt dizzy, light-headed.

"This is real," he said aloud. "This isn't a dream!"

I should not be able to hear these things!

He wondered what else he could hear, and strained to listen.

Cars. Rain. Faint music coming from a neighbor's house. A lot of voices, a lot of snoring. A baby crying. Footsteps slashing through the puddles. An almost silent *whip-whip-whip* sound that he couldn't place.

Then he heard Danny Cooper saying, "So we *are* going to Colin's house? He's probably in bed, Dad. I bet his parents are too. Can't this wait until morning?"

"No," Mr. Cooper said. "Trust me, this is important."

"Well, couldn't we have just phoned them?"

"This has to be done in person."

Colin got out of bed and looked out of the window. He could still hear Danny and his father talking, but couldn't yet see them.

He quickly dressed in a pair of jeans and a T-shirt, grabbed his sneakers from under the bed and went downstairs. His father woke with a start as Colin opened the door. "Dad, Mum? Something's wrong. Danny and his father are on the way over."

His father frowned. "What? I didn't hear the phone ring."

"They didn't phone. I can hear them talking." Colin sat down on the sofa to put his sneakers on.

"I don't understand. Why are they coming here?"

"Danny's father won't tell him."

"Are you sure you weren't dreaming, honey?" Colin's mother asked.

"Unless I'm *still* dreaming—and I don't think I am, am I?—I can hear them. I don't know how, but I can."

Caroline carefully put her book aside, got to her feet and stood in front of her son. "What *else* can you hear?"

Colin listened. "Everything. I can hear cats fighting, dogs barking . . . televisions, radios, car tires hissing on the wet roads . . . Mr. Johnston down at number 41 is complaining to his wife because there's not enough bread. He wants to make a cheese sandwich. She's just said that there's some bread in the freezer . . . He doesn't want to go to all that trouble . . . Now she's just said that *she'll* do it." Colin opened his eyes and saw that his parents were staring at him. "I'm not making this up!" He tilted his head to one side and listened. "I can hear so *much*. It's like being in a huge room packed with people who are all talking at once. And driving their cars and playing their radios."

"Concentrate," his mother said. "Focus on one specific sound and try to block out the others."

"OK. I can hear Danny and his dad talking. Danny's just asked his dad what they're going to do if we're all in bed. They're almost here. And there's something else in the background. It sounds kind of like a helicopter, only much quieter. Hold on." He concentrated again. "I think it's a couple of kilometers away, but it's getting closer. The pilot's just said something about track-ing a transponder. Whatever *that* is."

Colin's father started to speak, but Colin interrupted him. "The men in the helicopter . . . I think they're *following* Danny's father! They're talking about . . ." He frowned. "We've got to get out of here! Dad! They're coming for *us*! They're talking about making a clean capture!"

Colin's parents looked at each other and hesitated for a split second. Then Warren jumped to his feet. "Colin, go out and un-lock the car. Get in and put your seat belt on!"

"What?"

"Move! *Now!*"

"Dad, we'll never outrun a helicopter!"

"We're bloody well going to try!"

8

DANNY JUMPED BACK AS THE CAR ROARED
out of the driveway of Colin's house. "Where are *they* going?"

His father swore and pulled another device out of his canvas
bag. He spoke into it. "Green Montego, heading north from my
position! Stop it!"

"Dad? What's—?" Danny stopped. The wind had suddenly
picked up, gusting from behind, whipping the rain almost hori-
zontally ahead of them. A low, fast thumping sound came from
overhead. He turned to see an enormous black helicopter pass a
hundred meters above, pursuing Colin's parents' car.

Danny stared at his father. "What's going on?"

Without looking at him, Mr. Cooper said, "Be quiet."

"But . . ."

Mr. Cooper reached out and locked his hand around Danny's
arm. "I said, be quiet!" He glared at Danny.

Danny nodded.

"Danny, you always were a lousy liar. I *told* you not to tell
anyone about your powers!"

Colin clung to the back of his mother's seat as the car roared
around another corner. "Dad . . . !"

"We can do it!"

"The pilot's just been ordered to activate an infrared scanner."

Caroline Wagner shook her head. "We can't hide from that, Warren. Just pull over before you kill us all!"

Colin didn't know whether to be more shocked that they were being chased by a helicopter, or that his father was driving through the estate at four times the speed limit.

"They're going to try to corner us, Warren!" Colin's mother said. "Take the next left, through the Penrose estate!"

"We'll head into the underpass," Colin's father replied. "They can't follow us there."

"They'll just wait for us to come out the other side!" Colin said.

"I know . . . Colin, we're going to have to abandon the car, OK? We'll jump out and let it keep running. That'll give us a few minutes."

"Are you *crazy*? Mum! Tell him!"

"He's right, Colin." She was already undoing her seat belt.

"We'll be killed!"

Warren said, "Hold on! Roundabout!"

The car went straight over the roundabout, plowing through the flower beds that had been planted for Mystery Day—they were in the shape of the *T* on Titan's chest—and narrowly missed an oncoming motorbike.

Warren shouted, "We're nearly there! Colin, take off your seat belt and unlock the door!"

Colin did as he was instructed. Ahead, the entrance to the motorway's underpass was rapidly approaching.

As soon as the car was inside the tunnel, Warren hit the brakes. "Get out, both of you! And *run*!"

Colin and his mother jumped from the car, slamming the doors behind them. Then his father got out, pulled the small fire extinguisher from under the seat and wedged down the accelerator with it.

Still in neutral, the car's engine roared, but remained in place.

"Keep back!" Warren said. He leaned into the car, pressed down the clutch and forced the gearstick into third.

He released the hand brake and leaped back just as the car surged forward.

As Colin watched, the car shot out of the far end of the tunnel and kept going.

"Come on!" Warren shouted. They began to run back the way they had come. "I wedged the accelerator down, but it won't fool them for long."

Just before the entrance to the tunnel, they stopped at a steel door set into the wall. "Maintenance shaft," his father explained. "Access for the motorway's lights and the speed cameras. This comes out about two hundred meters away. Their infrared sensors won't be able to pick up our heat signatures in there." He pushed against the door. "Locked! Colin?"

"What?"

"Open this door!"

"If *you* can't open it, how am I supposed to?"

"Just try!"

Colin reached out, twisted the door handle and pushed. "I can't."

His father roared at him. *"Push!"*

Colin took a deep breath and threw his shoulder against the

door. There was a loud *crack* as the lock snapped and the door flew open. Colin tumbled through, landing heavily on his back.

Warren grabbed Colin's hand and hauled him to his feet. "Well done. Now, keep going!"

Colin stared at the ruined lock. "I don't believe I just did that!" He looked down at his trembling hands. He'd felt the resistance of the lock, but had somehow known that he was capable of exerting much more force than the lock could take. "How did I—?"

"Worry about it later, Colin," his mother said, pushing the door closed.

"There are no lights," Warren said. "We'll have to do this the hard way. I'll take the lead."

"There's light coming from *somewhere,*" Colin said, and he started to move forward. "I can see well enough."

He felt his father's hand grip his shoulder. "Lead the way, then."

"How did you know about this place, Dad?"

"The ambulance center got a call a couple of years ago. One of the maintenance workers collapsed down here. Colin, slow down a little. *We* can't see where we're going, but you seem to have enhanced night vision."

"How far are we along, Colin?" Caroline asked.

"About a quarter of the way, I think."

"Can you hear anything?"

"Well, I heard the car crashing, but that's all. Look, what's going on here? My hearing, my vision . . . and the door! How did I do that?"

"There's no time to explain, Colin!" his father said, nudging him in the shoulder. "Just keep moving!"

Colin stood his ground. "No! We're being chased by a bunch of guys in a helicopter and it's got something to do with Danny and his dad, and you know what's going on!"

He paused, suddenly realizing. "This is because of who Mr. Cooper used to be, isn't it?"

His father said, "So you know about Quantum?"

"Danny told me everything." Colin frowned. "But how do *you* know about that? Did Mr. Cooper tell you?"

"No, but then he didn't need to. Until ten years ago, your mother used to be Energy."

Colin stared at his mother in the half-light. "Is that *true*?"

She nodded.

Then Warren Wagner said, "And *I* . . . I used to be Titan."

Colin stared at his parents. "No *way*!"

"You're almost thirteen," his mother said. "That's the age when the superhuman abilities usually start to appear."

Colin's mouth had suddenly gone dry and he could hear his heart thumping like crazy. "So . . . I'm a superhuman? Really?"

"The powers aren't always inherited, so we weren't sure that it would happen to you," his father said. "Especially not after what happened on Mystery Day. Now look . . . Just keep going, Colin! I promise that we'll explain everything the first chance we get!"

Colin nodded, then realized that in the weak light his parents probably weren't able to see the movement. "OK . . ."

He turned and continued along the tunnel.

This can't be happening, he thought. *Maybe I am still dreaming!*

"Be careful," his father said. "The powers come and go at first. You won't be able to rely on them for a while."

Caroline said, "Colin . . . We wanted to tell you for a long time, but . . . we weren't sure. Sometimes the powers are passed on to the next generation, but usually they're not. Do you understand what I'm saying? The age of superhumans didn't end ten years ago at Mystery Day. It just . . . took a vacation."

"Watch it. There's a step down," Colin said. "So what happened?"

"Ragnarök had a machine. It was his last weapon, designed to strip our powers, to turn all superhumans back to normal. Ragnarök thought that he was shielded against it. He wanted to be the only one with any powers, but your dad had managed to break through the force field protecting Ragnarök. Your dad almost destroyed the machine but he was too late; Ragnarök activated it at the last second."

"Since then," Colin's father said, "there have been no superhumans, heroes *or* villains."

"What happened to the villains?"

"Most of them were caught and arrested," his mother said. "Some just faded back into normal life. Max Dalton told us that he didn't know whether Ragnarök's power-damper would also affect people who hadn't developed their powers yet."

His father said, "Colin . . . There are still a lot of people out there who would love to find out the real identities of the heroes. And none of the heroes have their powers now. There's no way for them to protect their families if anyone learns the truth. No matter what happens tonight, you can't let them know that you have powers too. Got that? If you mention *any* of this, you'll be putting a lot of people in danger."

"You can trust me," he said. "I doubt that anyone would believe me, anyway. It's really true, though?"

"It is."

"We're almost there," Colin said. "Duck your head, Dad. There's a bunch of pipes going across."

"Can you hear anything?"

"No . . . well, just traffic on the road above. Where do we go when we get out of here?"

"We'll have to get another car from somewhere. Something fast. After that, I don't know."

Colin stopped suddenly. "Wait . . . Damn it! They're waiting for us to come out! They've got both ends of the tunnel staked out!" He turned around to face his parents. "We're trapped."

The doors at each end of the maintenance tunnel burst open and Colin could see silhouetted figures rushing in.

Speaking softly and quickly, his father said, "Remember what I said, son! They can *not* find out that you're a superhuman!"

Colin swallowed, then nodded. Colin's mother just put her arms around him and hugged him close. She was shaking.

As the soldiers' flashlights approached, Colin felt his father's hand on his shoulder. "It'll be OK, Colin. Trust me. We have an advantage."

Then they were facing four large, heavily armed men in army uniforms.

"Stand apart from each other! Hands on your heads!" one of the soldiers shouted, his handgun raised and aimed at Caroline's head. "Any resistance and the woman dies!"

They were handcuffed and searched, then marched out of the tunnel.

The black helicopter had landed, its rotors still spinning silently.

They were forced into the copter, where Colin saw that Danny was unconscious, strapped into a seat. In front of him stood Mr. Cooper, a large semiautomatic weapon in his hands.

The man said nothing until the ramp had been pulled back into the copter and they were in the air. "Just . . . sit still, do as you're told, and all this will be over soon enough."

Warren swore at Mr. Cooper. "What the *hell* is going on, P.J.?"

"I was under orders to watch Danny and make sure that nothing happened to him." He turned back to Warren. "*You* probably would have been left alone, but Danny told Colin about his abilities."

Colin looked toward his mother. He'd never seen her with that expression before: pure rage. "You are *not* Paul Cooper! And you're certainly not Quantum. There's only ever been one superhuman with shape-shifting powers. You're Façade."

The man nodded. "Correct."

9

BLUE-WHITE LIGHTNING CRACKED ACROSS the lab's computer banks.

"Damn! It's overloading!" Victor Cross shouted. "Shut it down before we lose everything!"

One of the technicians raced toward the computers. "I'm trying!"

"Try harder!"

The technician began to pound furiously on the keyboard. "It's not happening! The system is locked out!"

Victor pushed him aside, then reached down and unplugged the computer from the power supply.

The computer sparked once, then was silent.

"Don't waste time trying to fix it," Victor said. "Just get the backup system online."

The phone on the wall buzzed and a woman's voice said, "Er . . . Mr. Cross? Some bad news."

Victor grabbed the phone. "What the hell did you do?"

"We ran a low-power test on the nucleus. There was some sort of leak. I don't know why, but it shorted out all the computers here. It shouldn't have had any effect."

"Well, it did. We lost our main computer here too. Who told you to test the nucleus?"

"No one, but we thought . . ."

He interrupted her. "You *didn't* think. If you'd thought, you'd have asked me first! What did we lose?"

"O'Brien and Hammond . . . They're alive, but badly burned."

"I'm talking about the equipment."

"Oh. Nothing that can't be replaced."

"Consider yourself lucky, then. I want you to assign two people to scour the entire base and see what effect your power surge has had. Make the security systems their top priority. The rest of you, repair everything and get back to work on the nucleus. I don't want any more time lost on this."

"Yes, sir."

Victor slammed the phone back into its cradle. He turned to the nearest technician. "Damage report?"

"I think that the data files are safe. The backup system will be online in a couple of minutes. What *was* that, anyway?"

"They think it was a leak from the nucleus."

The man's face drained of color. "Is that dangerous?"

"Only if you're a superhuman."

The energy surge had rippled through the entire complex. The technicians assigned to check for damage went through the complex level by level, room by room. A few computer components had short-circuited, but aside from that, the effect was minimal.

When they reached the storage room on level one, they opened the door, flipped the light switch and looked in.

"Nothing in here," one of them said. "Just a few old crates and that weird glass statue."

"It's not glass," his companion said. "Me and Kulvinder were moving it earlier and he slipped and it fell over the rail. Right down to level seven. Didn't get a scratch. If it was glass it would have broken into a million pieces. And then we had to carry the damn thing all the way back up here."

They closed the door and moved on.

A few seconds later, the door was opened again. The technician reached in without looking, turned off the light and closed the door behind him.

If he had looked, he would have seen that the statue of the girl had moved.

Colin was strapped into a seat, still handcuffed, sitting with his parents and Danny against the side wall of the copter. Danny was still unconscious, snoring softly.

Colin's enhanced hearing had returned a few minutes earlier. Now, he could hear the pilot talking to Façade.

"Fuel's getting pretty low," Colin whispered to his father. "We're going to be touching down to refuel any minute."

"Where are we?"

"Somewhere over the Atlantic," Colin said. "There must be an aircraft carrier or something."

His father said, "No, this is a Boeing CH-47 Chinook. It can set down on water." He nodded toward two large metal drums secured close to the cockpit. "It's my guess that they're reserve fuel tanks. They'll set down and switch over. They probably have enough fuel to get us to mainland America."

"What are they going to do to us, Dad?"

"I don't know."

Colin looked at Danny. "What about Danny's brother? If Façade has been pretending to be Mr. Cooper for so long, doesn't that mean that he's really Niall's father?"

"Yeah. It does."

The door to the cockpit slammed open and Façade stepped through. He crouched in front of Danny and pressed his index finger against the boy's neck.

"Leave him alone," Colin said. "Haven't you done enough?"

Façade turned to Colin. "I was checking that he's all right." His voice was soft, almost gentle, the same voice Colin had known for years, but there was a hard, determined look to the man's eyes. Façade stood back up and stretched. At that moment the copter lurched and he grabbed for the handrail to steady himself. "I haven't been in one of these things for a long time."

"So what happened?" Warren asked. "You were disguised as Quantum when Ragnarök's weapon was used and you weren't able to change back?"

"That's right."

"Can I ask you something?" Colin said.

Façade shrugged. "Go ahead."

"If you took over Mr. Cooper's life, then Niall is really *your* son, right?"

"Yes. He is."

"But you've left him behind."

"I know. But this is important."

"Won't you miss him?"

"I don't intend to be away forever."

Colin's dad asked, "Why are you doing this, Façade?"

Façade said, "Because it needs to be done. Danny was the oldest potential superhuman who hadn't developed any powers when Ragnarök's machine was used. I was ordered to watch him. I didn't expect that I would be doing it for so long. I certainly didn't expect to have to look like Quantum permanently. Once we all lost our powers I couldn't change back."

"What about Danny's real dad?" he asked. "What happened to him?"

"You don't need to know that."

"Then tell me this," Warren said. "Why did you wait? After the battle-tank, you could have abandoned your mission. Ragnarök was dead, there was no one to give you orders."

Façade said, "This is bigger than that, Warren. Bigger than you or me or any boy."

10

ONCE THE REPAIRS WERE UNDER WAY, Victor Cross went to the medical unit where he found Rachel examining Joseph.

"How's he doing?" Victor asked.

"Considering he's spent ten years in the same prison cell, he's in good shape physically. But mentally . . ." Rachel shrugged. "I don't know yet."

"Please don't talk about me like I'm not here," Joseph said. "Why *are* we here, exactly?"

Rachel regarded him for a second. "You don't know? I was told you knew more about this than anyone."

Joseph closed his eyes and rubbed his palm against his forehead. "Maybe once I did. Now . . . I've had ten years of memories and nightmares mixed together. I'm finding it hard to remember what was real and what wasn't." He inhaled deeply, relaxed and opened his eyes. "The boy . . . he'd be a teenager now, yes?" Before Rachel could respond, he continued. "Ah. Of course. You're bringing him here, yes? Façade has revealed himself."

"He's on the way. He's also bringing us Warren and Caroline Wagner and their son. He's almost thirteen years old."

"Yes, yes . . . He's a part of this too." Joseph smiled. "They called him Colin, if I remember correctly. What's their ETA?"

Victor said, "Eight hours. They're halfway across the Atlantic right now. They'll touch down at the base in Florida, take a civilian transport from there. Unfortunately, we put the country's defenses on high alert when we broke you out of prison."

Victor's cell phone beeped. He checked the display, then turned away from Joseph and Rachel to answer it. "Talk to me."

It was the electronic voice again. "I want you to contact the team in Orlando, get them ready. Make it clear to them that Daniel Cooper is not to be harmed in any way."

"Got it."

"How's Joseph?"

Victor left the room. When he was sure that Joseph couldn't overhear, he said, "He's having some trouble with his short-term memory—he keeps forgetting who we are—but he still remembers the important stuff. The drugs they were giving him in the prison are starting to wear off. He's becoming more lucid. I'm concerned that if he gets a full grasp of the situation he might not be so eager to cooperate."

"Just keep him doped up and under armed guard at all times. You know what to do if he gets out of control."

In the storage room on the top floor of the complex, where the glasslike statue had once stood, the girl was lying on the ground, curled into a ball, shivering.

She'd lain there for hours, unaware of anything other than the pain that coursed through her body.

She didn't know who she was. She didn't know what had happened to her. Her thoughts were a blurred jumble of images and words, memories and feelings.

Gradually, she became aware that one word was surfacing more frequently than any other.

Alive.

The pain finally began to subside. The girl pushed herself into a sitting position and looked around the dark room.

She reached up to her face and removed the small black mask from her eyes.

Renata Soliz spoke her first words in ten years: "I'm alive."

11

COLIN WOKE WITH A START AND REAL-
ized that the copter had touched down on land; its engines were
slowing down and he could hear vehicles approaching. At the
back of the copter, the ramp was lowered and sunlight flooded
in. The soldiers filed out, leaving their prisoners unsupervised for
the first time.

Colin looked at his parents and Danny. "What's the plan?"

"There is no plan, Colin," his mother said. "We're going to
have to do what they want and hope they let us go."

"That's crazy!"

"There's nothing else we *can* do," his father said, looking at
the handcuffs. "We don't even know where we are."

Colin listened to the copilot talking to Façade. "We're in
Florida. I think we're on a military base. They said something
about trucks to take us to the airport . . . they've got a private jet
waiting for us."

Warren said, "Colin, they don't know about your hearing.
That's the only thing that might give us an advantage. Keep listening. We might find out something useful."

"Wait . . . you can *hear* them?" Danny said to Colin.
"Seriously?"

"Later," Colin said.

Warren glanced at his wife, then turned back to the boys.

"We have to act as a team, OK? But sometimes . . . sometimes we have to act alone. Do you both understand that?"

They nodded.

"Good. If either of you sees an opportunity to escape, go for it. But only if you're absolutely certain that you can make it."

Two large troop carriers were reversed up to the Chinook's ramp. Colin's parents were herded into one, the boys were put into the other.

For the moment, Colin and Danny were alone. The heat in the truck was almost suffocating; the walls were too hot to touch and pencil-thin shafts of sunlight came through a series of tiny holes in the roof.

"All right," Colin said, speaking quickly. "We don't have much time, so just trust me, OK? You ever wondered how your parents got to know mine? It's because they used to work to-gether. My dad was Titan and my mother was Energy."

Danny snorted. "On any other day, that might seem strange."

"When you and your dad—I mean, Façade—were coming over to my house last night, I could hear you. Façade doesn't know I've got any powers, so we need to make sure he doesn't find out."

"What else can you do?"

"Not much. Not yet, anyway." He examined his handcuffs. "Before we were caught, I broke through the tunnel door and I could see where we were going even though there was no real light. I *should* be able to get out of these." He tensed his muscles, tried to concentrate, then strained against the cuffs.

"If you keep that up, the only thing you're going to break is your wrists," Danny said.

Colin relaxed his muscles. "My hearing keeps coming and going, so maybe my strength will come back. How about you?"

"Nothing," Danny said. "And even if my speed comes back, what good will it do me? I'll never get through the cuffs." He sighed. "I swear I'm going to make him pay for this. The first chance I get, I'm going to bash his skull in!"

"Dan . . ."

"I mean it, Colin! He pretended to be my father for *eleven years*! I don't even know if my real dad is alive! And what about my mother? She was asleep when we left the flat last night. She won't have any idea where we are. She must be going out of her mind with worry. And there's Niall . . . he's only seven years old! What's he going to think? Façade is Niall's father."

"Look, we don't know what they want you for, and your dad—Façade—he said something earlier about not being away forever. Maybe this won't be so bad."

"Then why did he have to kidnap us?"

Colin didn't have an answer for that one.

Danny said, "Did you notice the look in his eyes? He doesn't want to be here any more than we do. I think—"

"Wait!" Colin said, interrupting him. "My dad's saying something."

He concentrated, tried to focus on his father's voice.

"Colin . . . I hope you can hear me. Splitting us up was a mistake; now it's going to be harder to watch us. Most of these soldiers are greenhorns. I think this is the first action they've seen. When we get to the airport, maybe I can create some kind of diversion. It might be enough for you and Danny to get away. I don't think they're going to risk shooting you. But . . . they might threaten to shoot me or your mother. Don't believe them. They need us as much as they need you."

Colin was sure that his father was lying about that. He wished that he could somehow speak to him.

"If you do get away, be careful. We don't know how big this organization is; they could have spies everywhere. You need to get to Max Dalton. If you can't, then try to find a man called Solomon Cord. He will help you. Last I heard he was living in New York, but that's all I know. Colin, ten years ago Solomon Cord used to be Paragon."

He was about to tell Danny what his father had said when two soldiers—neither of whom Colin had seen before—climbed into the back of the truck and sat down opposite them, with their guns drawn.

A minute later, they were joined by Façade, who was now wearing civilian clothes. "How are you doing, son?" he asked Danny.

Danny swore.

Façade glared at him. "Watch your language." He sat down opposite them. "Either of you hungry?"

"Starving," Colin said.

"We'll get you something to eat on the plane."

"Let me phone my mother," Danny said. "She doesn't know what's happened. I want her to know that I'm OK."

Façade shook his head. "No. Sorry. I know you don't like it, and I understand that, but we can't do anything that might jeopardize this operation. Pretty soon it'll all be over. Then we can go home and forget about it, OK?"

"No. Not OK. Whatever happens, Façade, I will not forget this. I swear that I will make you pay for what you've done."

12

IT WAS A THIRTY-MINUTE DRIVE TO THE
airport, during which Colin discovered that army trucks were no
more comfortable than army helicopters.

As the truck stopped, Façade got to his feet. "We're taking
civilian transport, so we're going to have to pass through a few
public areas. Colin's parents are going first."

"What if we refuse?" Danny said.

One of the soldiers held up the pistol and turned it in the light
for them to see. "This is a ten-millimeter Auto Glock 20C. It's a
little lighter than the standard Glock 20." The soldier cradled the
gun as though it was a newborn kitten. "In my opinion, this is
the best handgun in the world."

Danny looked to the man he'd always thought of as his pro-
tector, his dad.

Façade turned away.

"You'll never get that thing through security," Colin said to
the soldier.

"Shows what *you* know, kid."

Façade said, "If anyone asks, you two are my sons. If either
of you tries anything . . . these men have been authorized to use
whatever force is necessary."

Colin, Danny and Façade walked through the packed airport,
flanked by the two soldiers who were doing their best to be in-
conspicuous.

Ahead, there was a long line at the security gate.

"Damn," Façade said. "This could take a while."

Colin could see his parents, accompanied by four plainclothes soldiers, in the line ahead.

"Go and see what the delay is," Façade said to one of the soldiers.

Colin glanced at Danny; they were now guarded only by Façade and the one remaining soldier. "Go!" Colin whispered. "Run! I'll try to stop them!"

Danny shook his head. "Can't. Too risky."

Then Colin heard his mother whispering to him. "Colin . . . Can you hear me?"

Colin nodded once, hoping that Façade wouldn't notice it.

"Good," his mother said. "Look to your left."

He looked. There was a gang of two dozen boys about his age being escorted by four stressed adults, probably their teachers. The boys were rushing about, talking, wrestling and generally causing chaos. As he watched, another two boys were deposited with the group by their parents, who looked relieved to have them off their hands.

Colin's mother said, "School trip, I think. We've been watching them for a few minutes. Their teachers are letting them go to the bathroom in groups of three or four. You might have a chance. Follow them in and see if you can swap clothes with one of them."

Colin nodded again and turned to Façade. "I need to go to the bathroom."

"You can go on the plane."

Colin looked around. Already, the line had filled up behind

them. He decided to take a chance. Loud enough for everyone around him to hear, he said, "I'm going to the bathroom, Dad. Keep my place for me."

He stepped out of the line and walked in the direction of the group of boys.

He listened carefully . . . Façade swore under his breath, then muttered, "Go after him, Davison!"

Colin could hear the soldier's distinctive footsteps behind him; the man was still wearing his army-issue boots.

He passed through the gang of boys and spotted one of their teachers, a pleasant-looking middle-aged woman. Taking a deep breath, he walked right up to her. "Can you help me? I can't find my parents." He did his best to look as though he was about to cry.

The woman gave him a friendly smile. "Do you know what flight they're on?"

"No."

"Well, where are you going?"

For a second, Colin's mind went completely blank and he couldn't think of the name of a single American city. "Um . . . New York."

"JFK or La Guardia?"

Colin didn't know what that meant, so he said, "JFK."

And then a heavy hand dropped onto his shoulder.

"There you are, Colin! I've been looking all over for you!"

He turned to see the soldier—Davison—smiling at the woman.

"Thanks," Davison said. "I thought we were going to have to leave without him!"

It's time to take another chance, Colin decided. To the woman, he said, "I don't know this man!"

Davison squeezed Colin's shoulder in a manner that probably looked friendly, but hurt like hell. "Oh, not this game again! It wasn't funny the last time, Colin."

The woman looked unsure.

"I'm sorry," Davison said to the woman. "He has a very inappropriate sense of humor."

One of the other teachers came over: a tall, well-built man in his thirties. Colin thought that he looked like a football coach. "Everything OK here, Mrs. Bergin?"

He looked Davison up and down.

Davison smiled even wider and pulled Colin closer to him. Colin could feel the cold metal of the gun pressing into his back.

"Everything's fine," Davison said. "My son here is just playing a little game." He lowered his voice and added, "He's a little slow."

Colin swallowed. "He has a gun. Tucked into his belt."

Davison beckoned the man closer. "Listen . . . The boy's got a hyperactive imagination. I blame his mother. She lets him watch James Bond movies."

By now, all of the boys and the other teachers had gathered around, wondering what was going on.

"I don't know . . . ," the teacher said.

Davison sighed, leaned close to the teacher's ear and whispered, "I'm Detective John Torres, Miami PD. The boy's father is currently awaiting trial for drug trafficking. I'm taking him to a safe house."

"Got any ID?"

Davison pulled his wallet out of the back pocket of his jeans, flipped it open and showed it to the teacher.

"Oh. I'm sorry, detective. It's just that when you spend thirty hours a week teaching kids of this age, you learn to pick up the signs. I could see that the boy was troubled."

"That's understandable," Davison said. He tucked his wallet back into his pocket. "Sorry about this."

Then Colin saw his chance: the teacher held out his hand to Davison, who shook it.

Colin twisted, spun out of Davison's grip, pushed his way through the group of boys and ran.

He didn't know where he was going, so he did the only thing that seemed logical; he ran toward the check-in desks, where hundreds of people were waiting in line. It didn't take long to lose Davison; Colin was a lot smaller and could easily slip through narrow gaps in the line where the soldier had to politely ask people to move aside.

Colin spotted a police officer and headed in his direction. As he approached the policeman, he glanced around and saw Davison slow down and pretend to be watching the display of flight departure times.

When he was sure that Davison wasn't looking in his direction, Colin turned and ran.

13

Now would be a good time to dis-cover I have flying powers, Colin said to himself.

He'd spent the past hour hiding under a truck on the top level of the airport's multistory parking lot. If Davison went to airport security and attempted to use the surveillance cameras to find him, it was unlikely that they'd spot him here.

His hearing—the only advantage he'd had over the soldiers—had returned to normal. The last thing he'd heard was Façade boarding the private jet with his parents and Danny, and telling them that Colin would be following on a later flight.

That gave him some hope; as long as Façade thought that Colin could be recaptured, the others were safe.

But Colin wasn't so sure that *he* was safe. He was alone in a country he knew little about, with no money, no food, only the clothes he was wearing, and absolutely no idea how he was going to get to New York to find Max Dalton or Solomon Cord.

He didn't even know how far away New York was.

I really should have paid more attention in geography.

Since Max Dalton almost never left his apartment in Manhattan, he was going to be easy enough to find, but almost impossible to get to. Colin decided that Solomon Cord would be a better bet.

He briefly toyed with the idea of coming out of hiding and finding Davison or the other soldier, on the grounds that there might be another, better chance to escape later.

Colin dismissed that idea almost immediately; if they caught him again, they'd watch him even more closely.

This is the only chance I'm going to get. I have to make the most of it.

He knew that the first thing he had to do was get away from Florida and to do that he needed money. If he could get enough to take a train or a bus to New York, he'd figure out what to do when he got there.

Then he realized that he couldn't take the risk of going to a bus depot or train station; Façade's men would almost certainly have people watching for him.

Colin wondered whether it might be possible to get out of the airport by tying himself under the truck, but a brief examination of the underside of the truck changed his mind; any vehicle with an undercarriage low enough that he couldn't be seen would make going over speed bumps rather painful.

He rolled out from beneath the truck, got to his feet and looked around for a car with New York license plates. He found only one, a hatchback that was more rust than car. Being a hatchback, the rear of the car wouldn't have concealed him even if he'd been able to figure out a way to open it. Besides, it seemed unlikely that the driver would actually be going to New York.

For about the hundredth time, Colin considered going to the police. It seemed to be the logical option, but his father had warned him that the organization that had kidnapped them would have spies everywhere.

He walked through the parking lot toward the elevators, where two groups of people were waiting. From the way they were clustered, Colin could see that they were not traveling together. He stood in the middle of the bunch, hoping that each group would assume he was with the other.

When the elevator finally appeared, Colin squeezed in and did his best to look as though he were supposed to be there.

He accompanied the families out of the elevator, along the walkway, toward the check-in desks, and found himself almost back where he had started.

There was no sign of Davison or any of the other soldiers, but he still didn't feel safe.

Colin joined another group of people, mostly adults, who were heading toward the main entrance, and settled in the middle of the group. There was much laughing, backslapping and handshaking going on, and a lot of the people—especially the older men—looked alike. This had to be some sort of family reunion.

This time, however, someone paid attention to him. A girl of about his own age fell in step next to him. She was wearing a pair of faded black jeans and a white T-shirt bearing the word "Scram." "Hi," she said. "You must be David. I'm Marie."

"Hi," Colin said, trying to keep his accent neutral.

"You're Steve's son, right? I thought he said you weren't coming."

"Change of plans," Colin said, wondering how long he could get away with this.

"The last time I saw you, you were about five." She looked at him closely. "You don't look much like your photos."

"Well, you don't look much like yours," he shot back.

She laughed. "God! Tell me about it! They always make me wear a dress and get my hair done for the pictures."

Colin felt that some sort of response was expected. "So, how old are you now?"

"Thirteen. Hey, where's your stuff?"

By now they were outside. The adults were gathered right in front of the entrance, joking and laughing, and completely oblivious to the other travelers who had to squeeze past them.

"My stuff?" Colin asked.

"Your bags and things."

"Steve has them." Colin thought, *I'm* not *going to get away with this.*

Marie said, "No, he's only got the one bag."

"Oh, damn. I must have left them inside." Colin ducked back into the airport. *Back to square one,* he thought.

Then the girl appeared next to him. "Hey!"

Colin turned to her. "Listen . . . I lied. I'm not David. I don't even know who David is. Or Steve, or any of them."

Marie stepped back, an amused look on her face. "Why would you do that?"

"You wouldn't believe me if I told you. The short version is that I have to get as far away from here as quickly as possible."

"Are you in some kind of trouble?"

"I'm in *every* kind of trouble."

"You're not American, are you? I can tell by your accent."

"No."

"Well, where are you trying to get to?"

"I need to find someone. An old friend of my father's. I don't even know where to begin."

"Well, he's in Florida, right?"

"I don't think so. Dad says that the last he heard, his friend was in New York."

Marie shook her head. "You've got a long way to go, then."

"I don't even know exactly where we are now."

"Jacksonville," Marie said. Seeing the blank look on his face, she added, "Northeast Florida. How could you not know that?"

Colin took a deep breath. "Look, I hate to ask you this, but can you help me? I've got no money, no clothes. Nothing."

"What happened to you?"

"Believe it or not, I was kidnapped. I got away from them, but they're still here somewhere, looking for me."

"Oddly enough, I *don't* believe you."

Colin had to smile. "I wouldn't believe me either. But it's true. Look." He reached into his pockets and emptied them. "See? No American money. Here's a receipt from my local shop. It has the address and everything. Look, we don't even use the same money as you do."

"So supposing it's true . . . What are you going to do?"

"I don't really know where to begin. Tell me this: if I knew someone's name, how would I go about finding him?"

"Duh! Use the phone! Call the operator. Or you could go to the cops."

"I'm not sure I want to do that."

"You're not saying that the cops are in on it too?"

"Probably not, but I can't take the chance."

Marie regarded him silently for a few seconds, then said, "OK . . . I'm going to trust you." She reached into her pocket and pulled out a ten-dollar bill. "This is all I have. I hope it helps."

"Thanks. I'll pay you back."

She smiled. "Really? How?"

Colin laughed. "You could give me your address and I'll send you the money when this is all over."

"I'm not *quite* dumb enough to give my address to someone I've just met." Marie took a pen from her pocket, wrote a phone number on the back of Colin's receipt and handed it to him. "Phone me."

"Thank you. I really appreciate this." He looked around. "I should get out of here."

They went back outside, where Marie's family were waiting for her.

"What's your name?" Marie asked quietly.

"Colin Wagner."

"Good luck, Colin. I hope it all works out."

"So do I. Thanks again."

He watched Marie and her family walk away, then walked in the opposite direction.

He had no idea what he was going to do next.

14

RENATA TRIED TO PIECE TOGETHER WHAT had happened to her, tried to understand how she had suddenly come to be in this place.

The last thing she could clearly remember was Josh Dalton kissing her on the forehead before he flew back into action.

A couple of minutes after that, one of Ragnarök's goons spotted her just as she spotted him. The man had raised his gun and fired, but not before Renata had changed into her invulnerable state.

The man had fired over and over, but the bullets had bounced harmlessly off her.

And then . . . what?

She didn't understand.

Until now, she'd always been fully conscious while she was in diamond form, aware of everything around her. She would always wait until she knew that it was safe before she reverted to her human form. But this time something different had happened.

One minute she'd been watching Ragnarök's henchman trying to find a way to hurt her and the next she was here, in this place, on the floor, wracked with pain.

So where the hell am I? she wondered. *Where's everyone else? Maybe Ragnarök has a teleportation device. Maybe he zapped me with it and sent me here.*

She went up to the door again and listened. A few minutes earlier, she'd heard two men talking nearby. Now, there was silence.

Renata carefully eased open the door and glanced out. She stepped out onto a wide metal walkway, one of many that were suspended around the edges of a large open area.

Some sort of cave. There has to be a way out other than by teleportation.

The complex was made up of a series of large caverns connected to each other by winding tunnels, corridors and stairwells. Each of the caverns was at least three stories high. There didn't seem to be any windows anywhere in the complex: no vents or doorways that led to the outside world.

Affixed to one wall Renata found a very old map that showed she was in an abandoned gold mine, but apart from that it wasn't much use; although a few of the old tunnels were still there, most of them had been filled in, replaced with newer tunnels that didn't match the map.

At the lowest level, Renata found a large, mostly empty cavern, four stories high, surrounded by levels and walkways. She was hiding in the shadows on a gantry close to the ceiling of the cavern.

So far she had managed to avoid being spotted, but she figured it wouldn't be long before someone went into the storeroom and realized that the diamond statue had gone. She knew that she should probably keep moving, but this was the best hiding place so far.

Below, at the very center of the cavern, was a large silver ball, two meters in diameter. It was spinning rapidly, floating unsupported in midair a meter above a large metal base.

What is *that thing?* she wondered.

A dozen technicians were working on the machinery that was connected by thick cables to the ball's platform.

Whatever it is, it's important, she decided.

As she watched, one of the technicians called out, "Mr. Cross? We're ready."

A young man in his early twenties approached. "I don't want any more power surges like the last one."

"That won't happen," the technician assured him.

"OK . . . Everyone step back. Laurie? Fire it up."

There was a brief flash of light and the ball began to rotate faster.

She heard the technician say, "Activating the null-field."

There was a second flash of light from the ball and the technicians all took another step back.

"It's steady. Three-meter radius, Victor."

Cross asked, "So who wants to test it?"

There were no volunteers.

"All right," the young man said. "I'll do it." He took a pen from his pocket and threw it at the ball.

The pen disappeared.

Renata crouched down, trying to get a better view.

"Looks like it's working," Cross said. "Let's see how close we can get." He took out a second pen and, holding it in front of him at arm's length, walked forward cautiously.

When he was about three meters away from the ball, the tip of the pen disappeared.

Renata watched as he pulled the pen back and examined the end of it.

"OK," Cross said, tossing the ruined pen aside. "We'll need the data from the kid before we can calibrate the nucleus. Everyone get some rest. It's going to be a long night."

When the last of the technicians had left, Renata silently climbed down to the floor, carefully avoiding the huge spinning ball.

She found the discarded pen and took a close look. It was as though an incredibly sharp knife had sliced off the nib.

Just as the man called Victor Cross had done, Renata held the pen out in front of her and slowly approached the nucleus.

She watched, fascinated, as the end of the pen disappeared.

So what's a null-field? she asked herself. Then she looked up at the silver ball. *And what's this all about? Why does it need such a lethal defense?*

Her stomach growled and she realized that she was hungry. She had a look around the room in the half hope that someone had left a sandwich lying around, but found nothing edible. There was a jacket hanging on the back of a swivel chair and Renata went through the pockets, but all she found was a folded newspaper. She was about to put the newspaper back when she spotted a familiar face on the front page.

It was Max Dalton.

That's not a good photo, Renata thought to herself. *It makes him look old.*

She unfolded the newspaper to read the article, then spotted the headline: "Mystery Day—Tenth Anniversary Exclusive!"

Mystery Day?

As she read the article accompanying Max's photo, Renata felt the hairs rise on the back of her neck.

"Maxwell Edwin Dalton—billionaire founder of MaxEdDal Pharmaceuticals—yesterday spoke out for the first time about the events of Mystery Day. Following his interview on *The Garth Russell Show,* Dalton held a short press conference. Reading from a prepared statement, he said, 'I wish to thank everyone for their support over the past ten years. I know that my siblings and I have remained silent and I realize how frustrating that may have been for many of you, but in our defense we lost some very good friends that day. We honestly do not know what happened when they went up against Ragnarök's battle-tank. Likewise, we don't know what happened to the other superhumans, be they heroes or villains.'"

This is impossible! Renata told herself. *It's a hoax. It* has *to be!*

She checked the date on the top of the page; it was ten years later than it should have been.

No, this is crazy! Someone's playing a trick on me!

But even as she thought that, Renata knew it couldn't be true.

She looked around the room, hoping to find something—anything—that would prove that the newspaper was a fake.

Because if it *wasn't* a fake . . .

None of Renata's family had known about her powers. Max had told her that they would be safer not knowing.

If it is *real, that means that as far as my family and friends know, I've been missing for* ten years!

Her hands shaking, Renata skipped to the end of the article: "In closing his statement, Dalton said, 'All that I can conclude is that superhumans—myself included—are an aberration. An inexplicable blip on the human race. The Earth was not designed for us, but for ordinary humans. Our time has now passed. My sister, my brother and I would like to leave those days behind us, leave the past buried with our friends Energy, Apex, Thalamus, Titan, Paragon and the others. Though our friends—and every other superhuman on the planet—are now long gone, they will not be forgotten. They will never be forgotten.'"

15

"I'M SORRY, SIR. I DON'T HAVE A PUBLIC listing for a Solomon Cord in New York," the operator said. "Your friend could be ex-directory."

"OK, thanks anyway," Colin said. He hung up the phone.

He was in a large shopping mall about seven kilometers west of the airport. According to the ornate clock that was set into a fountain in the center of the mall, it was one o'clock.

He still had the ten dollars Marie had given him, but—despite the hunger gnawing at his stomach—he refused to let himself buy any of the delicious-looking doughnuts from the café opposite the bank of phones.

Colin had managed to get this far only because of the free bus service from the airport to the mall.

As he was about to walk away from the phone, he spotted a poster offering to help out runaway kids. Beneath a photo of a wide-eyed little boy were the words, "Lost? Scared? We want to help! Call our toll-free number! 1-800-HERE-4-U. Confidentiality assured."

It's worth a shot, Colin decided. He phoned the number.

"We're here for you," a woman's voice said. "How can we help you?"

"I . . ." Colin stopped. He didn't know what he was going to say.

The woman assumed his hesitancy was fear: "Are you OK? Are you lost?"

"Sort of . . . Look, my name is Colin Wagner. I was kidnapped. I've escaped, but I don't really know where I am."

"I see. Where are you calling from?"

"A shopping mall. It's called The Twin Pines, or something like that."

"I know it. Do you want me to contact the police?"

"No! No, sorry, I don't trust them."

"Can you tell me why?"

"The kidnappers said that they had people working with the police."

"All right . . . ," the woman said. "How old are you? Where are you from? How did you escape?"

Colin told her a shortened version of his story—leaving out the truth about his parents' past—and finished with, "I have ten dollars. How far would that get me?"

"About as far as the door," she said. "If you want to get to New York on ten dollars, you'll have to go back in time about a hundred years."

Despite the seriousness of his situation, Colin couldn't help laughing at that. "What can I do?"

"If you really don't want to talk to the police, we can send someone to pick you up. They'll take you to a shelter for the night. At least you'll get a warm bed and a good meal. You can also talk to a counselor, if you like."

Less than an hour later, Colin was sitting on the edge of the fountain when he was approached by a short, fat, balding man. "Are you Colin?" he asked, sounding a little nervous. He pronounced it "Coe-lin."

Colin nodded.

"Hi. My name's Gene." He showed Colin an ID card. "I'm going to take you to the shelter. Is that OK?"

"Thanks," Colin said, getting to his feet. He was surprised to find that he was taller than Gene. "What did the woman on the phone tell you?"

"Just that you needed a lift. They tell us only the bare minimum. But you can feel free to talk to me about anything you like. I'm training to be a counselor."

They walked out into the parking lot. "You're not from around here?" Gene asked.

"No."

"That's fine."

Gene's car was a huge, brand-new sport-utility vehicle. He noticed Colin's expression. "Nice, isn't it?"

"It's great. My dad's car is about half this size." *Or was,* he added to himself.

"What sort of mileage does he get?"

"I've no idea."

Gene opened the passenger door and let Colin in. "This baby'll do twelve in the city, maybe sixteen on the open road."

"That's not bad," Colin said, though he didn't know whether it really was bad or good.

Gene climbed into the driver's seat and put on his belt. "OK, then. Let's go."

They drove out of the parking lot and—after a series of turns and junctions that Colin found completely baffling—onto the freeway. Colin felt weird, sitting in what he felt should be the driver's seat.

"So have you been doing this long?" Colin asked. "Helping kids, I mean."

"A couple of years," Gene said. "I took early retirement and needed something to fill my time." He turned to Colin and smiled. "I'm really only a driver, for the moment. But it's good work. Very satisfying."

"Do you have to pick up many people?"

"A couple a week. Though it gets a little worse around the holidays. Lot of kids can't take the pressure at home. That the case with you?"

"No, not really."

"That's fine." He paused. "You want to talk about it?"

"No, sorry."

"That's fine."

Colin couldn't help smiling to himself. Everything seemed to be fine for this man.

"You celebrate Mystery Day in your part of the world?"

"We do," Colin said. "Doesn't every country?"

"Yeah, I guess . . . We had a big parade in Jacksonville, lots of guys dressed up as superheroes. Most of them were Titan, of course. Here's a story for you: I met him once."

"You met Titan?"

"Sure did. He saved my life. This was . . . oh, about sixteen years ago. Remember a villain called Terrain?" Before Colin could answer, Gene said, "No, of course you don't. I forgot. You're too young to remember him. But you've heard about him, right?"

"I have."

"Well, I was working in construction at the time. We were

putting up an apartment complex. Expensive place, riverside view and everything. And there I am, working away—I was a plasterer—and the whole damn building begins to shake. We thought, 'Earthquake!' and we got out of the building as fast as we could. And outside we saw Terrain and Titan beating the living crap out of each other. Terrain was using his powers to throw cinder blocks and huge chunks of the sidewalk at Titan. Then he saw us standing in front of the building and he made this sort of gesture with his hand . . ." Gene held up his hand palm out, then clenched his fist and pulled back. "Next thing we know, the whole damn building is coming down. And Titan flies up to us, grabs hold of me and my buddy Carl and pulls us out of the way. We didn't even get a chance to thank him, because Terrain had split and Titan went after him. Pretty cool, eh?" Gene said.

"Yeah."

"Did you have many superheroes back home?"

"A couple."

"I wish I knew what happened to them. A lot of folks say that they were all killed, but I don't believe that. They couldn't've *all* been killed. What about the ones who weren't in Pittsburgh that day? Why haven't they shown up?"

"Maybe they decided to retire."

"Nah . . . How could you give up something like that? You know what my wife thinks? She thinks that they never really existed. She says that it was all a stunt rigged by the government to make all the crooks think that there was more to worry about than the cops. I say to her, 'Bridget, if they didn't exist, then I was flattened under a thousand tons of concrete and steel, and I've been *imagining* the past sixteen years.'" He laughed.

"If someone *was* making it all up," Colin said, "why would they stop?"

Gene nodded. "Good point. Good point."

"Do you know what happened to Paragon?"

"Oh, that guy. Bridget calls him 'the creepy one,' 'cause of how he used to just sort of skulk around in the shadows. I guess he went the same way as the others, whatever that was."

"It's just that I've been thinking about him a lot . . . If all the superhumans died or just disappeared, then what about their secret identities? Wouldn't there be people thinking, 'I haven't seen Uncle Pete since the day all the heroes disappeared'?"

"You're a smart kid, Colin."

"Thanks."

"You doing OK in school?"

"About average."

"Got any brothers or sisters?"

"There's just me." Colin decided to switch the conversation away from himself. "What about you? Any children?"

"We have a son in medical college. He's getting married after he graduates. A real nice girl, she is. I have to tell you, I'm real proud of him. I should have done something like that, you know? Something to help people."

"My dad's a paramedic," Colin said.

"Yeah?" Gene steered the car onto the freeway's exit ramp. "Good work, that. What about you? Are you going to follow in your father's footsteps?"

"I hope so." Colin couldn't help wondering where his parents were now, whether he'd ever see them again.

The task ahead of him seemed impossible.

A week ago all I had to worry about was getting my homework done and remembering when it was my turn to peel the potatoes.

His mouth was suddenly dry; Colin felt as though he were trying to swallow sand.

Now I'm on my own in God-knows-where and my parents and my best friend have been taken hostage. What if they're already dead?

"Hey," Gene said. "You OK, Colin?"

Colin brushed the tears away from his eyes. "Yeah, I'm OK. Allergies."

"Uh-huh . . . You sure you don't want to talk about what's going on?"

"I wish I could. But . . . it's complicated. Sorry."

"No, no, that's fine. We're here to make things easier for young people like yourself, not to make things harder! You don't have to tell me anything you don't want to." Without pausing, Gene changed the subject: "It'll take us about thirty minutes to get to the shelter. Traffic is crazy downtown. It's been getting worse the past few years." They turned right into a residential area, where they made another complicated series of turns.

Colin was looking out of the window. "Some of these houses are huge!"

"Yeah, this is what you might call an upmarket area. I have to tell you, Colin, the shelter is not in the best part of town. It can be a pretty rough area. Fact is, I'm going to park half a mile or so from the shelter. You don't mind walking the rest of the way?"

"No. Listen, thanks for this. I can't pay you back."

"You don't owe me anything. We're here to help. I mean, if

my boy was in trouble, I'd like to think that there would be someone he could turn to for help."

Eventually, Gene steered the car into the parking lot of a
small mall, found a spot and shut off the engine. "OK . . . Colin,
you ever spend the night in a shelter before?"

"No."

"Right. There's a few things you should know. You're about
twelve or thirteen, right? Well, most of the other kids are fifteen,
sixteen, some are older. They can be pretty tough. When we get
there, I'm going to hand you over to one of the helpers. You
stick with them, do exactly what they say, OK? If any of the
other kids give you trouble, try to get to one of the helpers. If
there's no one around, whatever you do, don't accept anything
from the other kids. You got that?"

Colin nodded.

"I'm serious. Don't eat, drink or smoke anything they give
you, no matter what they say. The bad kids tend to hang around
in gangs of three or four. They'll want to check you out. Best
thing to do is say as little as possible. Don't make eye contact if
you can avoid it. They call you any names, don't respond."

"OK," Colin said. "Thanks."

"Let's go, then."

16

DAVISON HANDED FAÇADE THE LEAR JET'S satellite phone. "It's Victor Cross."

Façade carried the phone toward the front of the plane, out of earshot of the passengers. "What do you want, Cross?"

Victor Cross yelled, "How the *hell* did you let him get away from you? He's just a kid!"

Façade said, "He's smart, and I think he's more than just that. When we got to the Wagners' house, they already knew we were coming. And he got away from Davison. Consider who his parents are."

"You still have *them,* right? You're not going to tell me that they escaped as well?"

"They're here. And Danny."

"So you think that Colin has inherited?"

"His parents deny it, but considering that Colin is the offspring of *two* superhumans, well, you do the math."

"That would make him more important than any of them. You realize that? What are you doing to find him?"

"We've still got the airport staked out, but it's unlikely he's still there, less likely that he'll return. If we knew what his plans were, we'd have a better chance of finding him."

"Do I have to think of everything? Interrogate his parents. Find out from them where he might go."

"They don't know he's missing yet. They think he's following us on another flight. If I tell them he's missing, they'll be even less cooperative."

"Façade, the chances are that they've already figured it out. The other boy will have told them."

"No, I've kept them separate. Look, don't go dumping this on me. They're your people. You hired them. If they're as good as they're supposed to be, they'll find Colin."

"They'd better. If he talks to the authorities, he could destroy this entire operation. Certain people will *not* be pleased about that, you understand me? And I'll make sure that they're aware that you're responsible. You were undercover for eleven years. No one knows you and no one will care if your corpse turns up in a Dumpster somewhere."

Façade paused. "When this is done, Cross, you and I are going to have words. Do *you* understand *me*?"

"You have to eat," Rachel said to Joseph. "You've barely touched your soup!"

Joseph pushed the tray of food across the desk. "It tastes like crap. I had better food in the prison. I feel like I'm going to throw up."

I'm not surprised, Rachel thought. *I'd be sick too, if I was forced to eat that garbage.* "It's loaded with proteins and vitamins, Joseph. You need to get your strength back. Just eat it."

Joseph looked at her, then at the tray of food. He pulled the tray back and resumed eating.

Since his rescue from the prison, Joseph had grown stronger

and more focused, and had begun to question Rachel's orders. Now, in order to keep him docile, everything he ate or drank was drugged with a low dose of thiopentone sodium. It had the added effect of making him very obedient.

A device on Rachel's belt beeped twice. She unclipped it, flipped open the cover and examined the tiny screen.

"What's that?" Joseph asked.

"It's a palmtop."

"A what?"

"A computer. It's a progress report from Victor. The last of the equipment has arrived."

Joseph said, "So who *is* Victor Cross?"

"He's smart. He's exceptionally good at figuring people out. That's why he was hired. He's one of those people who are able to get things done."

"I've seen the way you look at him—"

Rachel interrupted him. "Eat your food."

Joseph resumed eating. Around a mouthful of food, he said, "It tastes wrong."

"Just eat it."

He looked down at the carrot he'd speared on his fork. "It's drugged, isn't it? You've put something in the food to make me more amenable."

"Eat," Rachel said.

Joseph put the carrot into his mouth and chewed. "I don't like this. I've had enough of people trying to control me. I thought those days were over."

"It'll *all* be over soon."

"I know what happens to you, Rachel."

"I don't want to hear this."

"Your people broke me out of prison because you need my knowledge of the future. I don't know everything, but I do know how it ends for you. I've seen your death. It's not pleasant."

17

GENE HAD LEFT COLIN IN THE CARE OF a tiny, fierce-looking young woman who introduced herself as Trish. She looked about twenty, with large brown eyes, bright orange spiky hair and a face covered in piercings. There was a large silver ring through her lower lip that rattled against her teeth when she talked.

But despite her slightly menacing appearance, Colin soon discovered that Trish wasn't scary; she had a soft, pleasant voice and a permanently cheerful smile.

She directed him into her office and pointed to a chair that was against a blank wall. "Have a seat. I want to take your picture, OK?"

"Why?"

"Officially, it's because we're supposed to keep records on all the kids who pass through here. Unofficially, it's because in my experience most of you give false names and you can't remember which name you used last time. We don't mind false names, but we will want to know who you are if you turn up again. So, if you don't mind?"

Colin sat down. "Go ahead."

Trish unlocked her desk drawer and took out a Polaroid camera. "OK . . ." She snapped a shot. "One more for luck . . . OK. Great, thanks." She locked the camera and the photos in the drawer and sat down at the desk. "Drag the chair over here, Colin. Is this your first time somewhere like this?" she asked.

"Yeah," Colin said, lifting the chair into place.

"OK . . . We need to do some paperwork now. Is that all right?"

"Sure."

"You want a soda or anything? Hungry?"

"I'm starving. I can't remember the last time I had something to eat."

Trish unlocked her desk drawer again and removed a bag of cookies. "Help yourself."

"Thanks!" Colin greedily grabbed the bag and opened it. The smell of chocolate cookies made his stomach growl, and he wolfed them down.

"What's going to happen next?" he asked.

"Next?"

"I mean, how long will I be here?"

"You're not under arrest or anything, Colin. You can come and go whenever you like. But since you're under age, I'm going to have to make a report to Welfare. They'll send someone in a day or two to talk to you, try to get you back in touch with your family."

"The problem is I haven't run away from home. The woman I was talking to on the phone didn't tell you?"

"No, they just tell us your name and where to pick you up. So what happened?"

"I was . . ." Colin was tempted to say "abducted," but that could lead to a whole new set of problems. "I was just separated from my parents. I'm lost."

"How did that happen?"

"We had to change flights at the airport. We weren't able to get seats together. When the plane landed, my parents got off and I didn't realize. I was waiting for them to come to me, and when I realized that the whole plane was empty, I went looking for them."

Trish regarded him silently. "So why didn't you stay at the airport?"

Damn!

"OK . . . I'll tell you the truth. I was kidnapped."

"Uh-huh."

"Really, I was. We all were. I escaped, but they've still got my parents and my friend. They told me that they've got people everywhere, even in the police, so I can't go to them."

Trish leaned forward and rested her chin on her hands, staring into his eyes. "Why were you kidnapped?"

"It's a long story."

"I've got the time."

"It's a long story that I don't want to tell."

"All right . . . Colin, you realize that we can only help you if you cooperate with us?"

"I understand that."

"I'm going to have to assume for the moment that you're telling the truth. If you can't go to the police, how do you expect to help your parents?"

"There's a man I need to contact. He used to know my parents. He'll help."

Trish leaned back, picked up a pencil and began to twirl it around her fingers. "And how do you know he'll be able to do anything?"

"He used to be . . . good at that sort of thing."

"What was he, in the FBI, the ATF or something?"

"I think so."

"I see. And how are you going to find him?"

"I have no idea. I don't even know where to begin."

"You do know his name, though?"

"Yeah." Colin dipped his hand into the bag for another cookie and was surprised to find that the bag was empty. "Sorry. I ate them all."

"I'll live." Trish pulled her computer keyboard over and started tapping at the keys. "We've got links into the largest databases in the world. If your parents' friend is registered anywhere, we'll find him."

"OK. His name is Solomon Cord. I don't know how to spell it, though."

"Doesn't matter. This thing is good at matching names by the way they sound, not just the way they're spelled. Now, what's your last name again?"

Colin said, "Wagner," and then realized that he'd been tricked; he'd been planning to give her a fake last name.

Trish nodded and started tapping at the keys. "I've found twenty-four Colin Wagners in this state . . . Five of them are about your age. None reported missing."

"I'm not from this state. I'm not even from this country. Can't you tell by my accent?"

"Colin, we get all sorts of people in here. Half the time I can't understand their words, let alone worry about their accent. All right, let's find your friend. Any idea how old he is? Middle name? Location? Current occupation? Race? Religion?"

Colin shrugged. "He's probably about . . . I don't know. Forty,

forty-five. I wouldn't think he's much older than that. I've no idea what his middle name is or what he does. I know that he was in New York at one stage. Oh, and he's black."

"You're not giving me much to go on." A minute later, she smiled. "OK . . . I've got one. He's not in New York, but it might be your friend. And there's a driver's license photo." She turned the monitor around to show Colin, holding her hand over part of the screen to block out the rest of the information. "That him?"

Colin peered at the photo. This Solomon Cord looked a little older than his father, a handsome man with strong features. Colin tried to picture the man wearing the armor and visor of Paragon. "That could be him."

Trish swiveled the monitor back. "If this address is right, he lives in Richmond, Virginia."

"Is that far?"

She smiled. "Oh yeah. Over six hundred miles."

"How can I get there?"

"You can't. I'm not allowed to give you any more details than that. But what I can do is get in touch with our affiliates in Richmond, ask them to visit Mr. Cord, give him the phone number here. It could take a couple of days. You feel up to staying around that long?"

"Sure. Thanks."

Danny woke up suddenly as the Lear jet touched down. He was in a tiny cabin at the rear of the jet, his hands still cuffed. A soldier was sitting directly opposite him, staring at him.

"Where are we?" Danny asked.

The soldier ignored the question.

"What happened to Colin? Aren't you allowed to talk to me?"

The soldier just continued to stare.

All right, Danny said to himself. *Now, concentrate! I can't get out of these cuffs, but maybe I can speed up enough so that I can search him for the key without him even noticing.*

He tried to focus only on his speed, to alter his perception of time so that everything around him was moving slowly.

It didn't work.

Five minutes later, Danny was escorted off the plane and toward a waiting car. He looked around. This wasn't an airport, just a small airfield. There were no other planes, no other people around.

"Where are we?" he asked Davison.

"No talking."

"Really? Funny name for an airfield."

Davison laughed. "Smart kid," he said to Façade.

Façade stared back, his face grim. "Just put him in the car and make sure that he doesn't get a chance to talk to Colin's parents."

Danny said, "You haven't caught him, have you? That's why you kept me and his parents separate on the plane. They don't know for sure that he got away."

"It won't make any difference, Danny," Façade said. "Colin's on the other side of the country. He doesn't know anyone in America, and he has no idea where we are. I don't rate his chances."

"If anything happens to him, Façade, I'll make you pay."

Davison laughed again. "How? You're tied up, surrounded, and your powers don't work. What are you going to do? Talk us to death? Now, get in the car."

"Colin's still free. He'll find a way to stop you."

Façade said, "You have to face the truth, Dan. Colin's gone."

18

COLIN WAS SHARING A ROOM WITH FOUR
other boys who all looked about fifteen or sixteen. They seemed
friendly enough, but kept the conversation to a minimum. Colin
assumed that this wasn't so much because they weren't curious
about him, but more because they didn't want to answer questions about themselves.

The room had two triple bunks and Colin was told that he
could have one of the top bunks. He thought that this was a
friendly gesture, since everyone would want the top, but almost
immediately he discovered that it was the *least* desirable bunk, because every time one of the other boys moved, the whole bed
shook.

It was late afternoon and Colin had been trying—without
success—to get some sleep. The boy lying on the bunk beneath
him was reading a comic book and kept laughing out loud.

Finally, Colin gave up trying to sleep. He leaned over the
edge of the bunk. "Hi."

The other boy glanced up at him, nodded and resumed reading. He was wearing a plain blue T-shirt, faded jeans and sneakers without socks. He didn't look much older than Colin, but his
worn clothes and rough hands suggested that this wasn't his first
time in the shelter.

The boy had a small pile of other comics beside him.

"What're you reading?" Colin asked.

The boy showed him the cover. The comic was called *Sprout*.

"Any good?"

"Yeah, it's pretty funny."

The boy seemed harmless enough, even a little nervous. "My name's Colin."

"Nick."

"So why are you here?"

Nick paused. "Why are *you* here?"

Colin laughed. "Ah . . . I think I'm beginning to understand this place."

Nick put his comic aside. "Your first time?"

"Yeah."

"How old are you?"

"Thirteen. Nearly."

"God . . . I thought *I* was the youngest. I'm fourteen."

Colin swung down from the bunk. "Have you been here long?"

Nick propped himself up on his elbow. "Three days, so far. They'll probably come for me tomorrow."

"Who?"

"My mother and her boyfriend. What about you? Who are you running away from?"

"No one. I'm trying to find someone."

"That's a first. Most kids here are running away."

Colin lowered his voice. "Some of them look pretty tough."

"You learn how to take care of yourself. Or at least, you learn how to *look* like you can take care of yourself. You got the time?"

"No. Sorry."

"It must be close to four. What are you on?"

"On?"

"Your chores. Didn't Trish give you anything to do?"

"No."

"That's probably because this is your first day. We're supposed to help out, you know? It's part of the whole 'being treated like an adult' thing. I'm on kitchen duty. Supposedly, we'll learn responsibility." He paused. "It doesn't work, but it passes the time. If you've got nothing else to do, you can help me."

"Sure."

Nick climbed out of the bunk and stretched. He gathered up his comics, then paused. "Stuff like this is a kind of currency here. I have to make sure that no one's going to find them."

"You want me to wait outside while you hide them?"

"Yeah."

Colin left the room and closed the door behind him.

The wide corridor had seven other doors, which Trish had told him led to other bedrooms. "We can accommodate up to fifty people," she'd said. "Though it's very rare that we're full."

At the end of the corridor was a large open area where sunlight poured in through a huge window, in front of which four older boys were stretched out on a pair of very battered sofas. Colin glanced toward them and realized that one of them— larger and older than the others—was looking back. The boy looked about seventeen or eighteen. He was pale-skinned, wearing a new black leather biker's jacket, with long, ragged blond hair spilling down over his shoulders, and a goatee.

Behind Colin, Nick came out of the room and saw the other boys. "Oh crap. Come on."

Colin followed Nick down the stairs, through the hallway and into the kitchen.

At one end of the large kitchen, two boys were peeling a mountain of potatoes. They were engrossed in whispered conversation.

"Who are those guys upstairs?" Colin asked.

Nick rolled up his shirtsleeves and pulled on a pair of rubber gloves. "That's Razor's gang. You don't want to mess with him." He handed Colin a dishcloth that featured a faded map of Australia. "You're drying, OK?"

"OK."

"Razor's been on the streets since he was eleven, I heard. He's seventeen now." Nick began to sort through the dirty dishes. "I hate this! Everyone's supposed to rinse off their dishes when they've finished their lunch, but almost no one does!" As the sink filled with hot, foamy water, Nick gave Colin a sideways glance. "Here's a tip. In a shelter like this, the kitchen is a dangerous place. Lot of sharp edges and hot surfaces. Accidents can happen. You know what I'm saying?"

"It's not the place you want to be if someone's got a grudge against you."

"Exactly. And grudges can happen for absolutely no reason. So . . ." He picked up a large bread knife. "You wash things like this *last*. Keep it next to you."

Colin paused. "It's that bad?"

"It can be." He smiled. "Relax, will you? This is one of the better places. One time I was in a shelter in Tallahassee . . . Guy about my age got his face burned off over the stove. He made the mistake of sitting in the wrong chair in the TV room. Another guy accidentally fell down the stairs four days in a row." Nick dumped a large pot into the sink and began scrubbing it.

"Why doesn't anyone *do* something?"

"Jeez, you *are* a novice. You report it to the staff and next thing you know you're getting the crap beat out of you every day. You have to let these things go."

He handed the pot to Colin.

Behind them, the door to the kitchen crashed open. Colin turned to see Razor and his gang watching him.

The two boys peeling the potatoes suddenly remembered they were supposed to be elsewhere and ducked out of the room.

Nick swore under his breath. He grabbed the bread knife and held it under the water.

Razor said, "Hey! New boy! What're you looking at?"

Colin swallowed. "Nothing."

"We just thought we'd say hello. Welcome you to this place."

"Thanks."

"You want to shake on it?" Razor held out his hand.

Colin glanced at Nick, who was giving all his attention to the dishes.

"You don't need to ask his permission," Razor said. "What's your name, new boy?"

"Colin."

Again, Razor held out his hand. "Nice to make your acquaintance, Colin."

Tentatively, Colin reached out. Razor's hand was almost twice the size of Colin's.

Colin felt a shock of pain along his right arm as the older boy began to squeeze.

"What's the problem, new boy? I'm not hurting you, am I?"

Colin gritted his teeth. "No."

He could feel the sweat building on the back of his neck.

"That's good. I wouldn't want to hurt you." He squeezed harder; Colin could feel the bones in his hand grinding together.

Razor's friends laughed. One of them said, "Hey, Raze! I don't think he likes shaking hands with you."

Razor frowned. "That so? Is that the case, new boy?"

"No."

"So you're calling my friend a liar, are you?"

Enough is enough, Colin said to himself. *I didn't escape from Façade and his men just to get beaten up by a gang of kids only a bit older than me!* "Let go of my hand."

"Now, that's not very friendly!" Razor said. "You've hurt my feelings. What are you going to do to make up for it?"

"Nothing," Colin said. "You're tough. You'll get over it."

Razor suddenly laughed and his grip relaxed a little. "I think I like you, new boy. You've got guts. Either that, or you're extremely stupid." He increased the pressure, his fingernails cutting into the back of Colin's hand.

"I'm beginning to think that I'm extremely stupid. Now, please, let go. You've made your point."

Razor considered this. "I heard 'Please,' but I want to hear 'Pretty please.'"

Colin's hand ached with the pain. His head was spinning and he felt like he was going to throw up.

Then every muscle in Colin's body suddenly flinched.

Razor laughed. "You sure I'm not hurting you, new boy?"

And then the pain in Colin's hand and arm was gone, but he could see from the taut tendons in Razor's wrist that the boy was still squeezing as hard as he could.

Colin smiled. "Last chance, Razor. Let go."

"You telling me what to do?"

"Yes."

"I don't think I will. I want to hear you begging for mercy."

Colin tensed his muscles and squeezed back.

Razor's grin faded. "No . . . !"

The hand felt like loose clay in Colin's grip. He squeezed harder.

Razor gasped, his eyes widening. "Jesus! Let go!"

"You hurt *my* feelings," Colin said.

Two of Razor's friends grabbed Colin's arms and tried to pull him away. Colin gave one last squeeze and Razor dropped to the floor, his eyes rolling, his skin covered in a film of sweat.

Colin let go of Razor's hand and looked at the boy on his left, who was now backing away. "Hi. My name's Colin. Shake?" He reached out his hand.

Razor's gang hesitated for a second, then disappeared from the room. Colin reached down, grabbed Razor's arm and hauled him easily to his feet. "Go away," Colin said.

Razor turned and ran.

Colin looked around to see Nick staring at him.

"How the hell did you do *that*?"

"It's an old family trick," Colin said, smiling.

19

HIDING IN THE SHADOWS ON A GANTRY high above the mine's entrance cavern, Renata Soliz watched as the huge steel doors rolled shut.

She sighed. She'd been hoping for an opportunity to make a run for it, but the entrance was continually swarming with armed soldiers.

The two large cars that the soldiers had recently escorted in now came to a stop. The door of one of them opened and an unconscious, handcuffed teenage boy was pulled out, lowered onto a stretcher and carried down a side corridor.

Renata thought that there was something familiar about the boy, but she couldn't place it. *Besides,* she reminded herself, *if it's true that ten years have passed, then there's no way I'd know him.*

She was now convinced that the newspaper hadn't been a fake; she'd found other newspapers, diaries, calendars, even coins. They all confirmed that she'd been gone for ten years.

The newspaper articles also made it clear that all of the superhumans had disappeared during the battle with Ragnarök. What didn't make sense was the fact that in the newspapers Max Dalton denied that The High Command had been involved in the battle.

Renata knew they *had* been there, but somehow they were still around.

Maybe I didn't disappear because I was solid. Maybe whatever it was that affected the others couldn't affect me in the same way; it just put me in some sort of stasis. So what woke me up?

The doors to the second car were opened and a middle-aged couple—also handcuffed—were taken out.

Renata gasped silently when she suddenly recognized the woman.

Oh my God! It's Energy! *She's alive! And that must be Titan . . .*

She'd never seen Titan without his mask, but this man was very much like him. The same build, the same hair color— though now it was graying at the temples and receding a little.

As she watched, Titan and Energy were escorted down the same corridor.

So why don't they do *something?* Renata wondered. *Why don't they just break the handcuffs and escape?*

She looked around the rest of the cavern; there was no one about.

Moving as quietly as she could, Renata made her way to the nearest stairway, ran down the stairs two at a time and dashed toward the corridor.

The ability to transform herself into a solid, unmoving object was great for defense, but not much good for attack.

Well, there's one *way to do it.*

Ahead of her, three soldiers were directly behind Energy and Titan.

Renata ran as fast as she could and leaped forward, changing to solid form in midair.

She slammed into the nearest soldier, knocking him to the ground.

The other two spun toward her, raising their weapons. Renata switched back to human form, lifted up the fallen soldier and held him in front of her as a shield.

"Shoot—and you'll kill your own man!"

One of the soldiers grabbed Titan and pushed the barrel of his gun into his chest. "Let him go, girl, or this man dies. You have three seconds. One."

"Titan!" Renata shouted. "*Do* something!"

"I can't," Titan said.

"Two."

"Our powers are gone," Energy said.

"Thr—"

Renata threw the soldier to the ground and stepped back.

The one who had his gun in Titan's chest unclipped a walkie-talkie from his belt. "Get Cross down here. We have a situation. Another superhuman."

20

LYING IN HIS BUNK, COLIN COULD HEAR Trish in her office downstairs, talking on the phone to a colleague in Virginia.

It was ten o'clock in the evening. Colin's enhanced hearing had returned shortly after the incident with Razor and his gang in the kitchen. Since then, it had been coming and going seemingly at random, though it was working more often than not.

Colin could hear almost everything around him, and he was learning how to focus on specific sounds. That was how he could hear not only Trish on the phone, but also her colleague, a man called Jonathan who had a whiny, nasal voice.

Trish read out Solomon Cord's details—including his address—to Jonathan. "The kid seems genuine," Trish said. "I don't think he's making it up."

"How old is he?"

"Thirteen, he says. Looks it too. One of our guys picked him up at a mall a few miles from the airport. The thing is, I checked with the airport and there's been no report of anyone missing."

"All right . . . Have you checked with the police?"

"No. He was pretty insistent about that."

"Trish, he's only thirteen! If he says he was kidnapped then that's just cause for breaking the confidentiality rule! You're supposed to report it!"

"I know . . . but I thought I'd give him a couple of days."

"Yeah? And suppose his folks come looking for him and they

find out that he's been in your care and you didn't report it? They'll sue your ass off."

"I know, but . . ."

Jonathan interrupted her. "Trish, the last thing your shelter needs is more bad publicity. I'm telling you to follow procedure on this one. Phone the cops and Welfare. If you don't do it, I'll have to go over your head. You don't want that, do you?"

Trish sighed. "No. No, I don't." She said good-bye and hung up. There was a long pause, then she picked up the phone again.

After a dozen rings, a voice on the other end said, "Jacksonville PD, front desk."

"Yeah, hi. This is Trish Jamison over at the mission shelter. I need to speak to someone about a kid we brought in today."

Colin decided he'd heard enough. He rolled off the bunk and landed silently on the floor, pulled on his clothes and sneakers and left the room.

He could hear Nick downstairs in the TV room chatting with a group of other boys and a few other quiet conversations in other parts of the shelter.

There was no one in the hallway downstairs.

He quickly considered his options. He could stay, and hope that Façade didn't have anyone working in the local police force, or he could run, but that didn't seem like the wisest option. He still had the ten dollars that Marie had given him at the airport, but apart from that, he was no better off than he had been earlier.

No, that's wrong, he thought. *Now I know Solomon Cord's address.*

Colin went downstairs, ducked past the partly open doorway to Trish's office and into the kitchen.

He found an old canvas shopping bag and filled it with as much food as he could find, telling himself that it wasn't really stealing, because when all this was over, he'd pay them back.

Then he heard a car engine coming to a halt outside the building. Two men were in the car, one of them on a cell phone.

"Yes, sir," the man with the phone said. "We're here. How old is the boy?"

"About thirteen," said a man's voice on the other end of the call.

"Got that."

"Move fast. The real cops are already on the way over. You've got ten minutes, tops. Don't screw this up. Any means necessary, understood?"

"Understood, sir." There was a faint beep as the man disconnected the call. To his passenger, he said. "Let's move. Boy's name is Colin Wagner, age thirteen . . ."

Then Colin's hearing returned to normal and all he could hear was his own panicky breathing.

Colin frantically looked around the kitchen: there were heavy bars on the windows and no other door. There was no way out.

Unless . . .

Colin grabbed his bag and walked out into the hall. He quietly opened the front door, just as two large, well-dressed men were coming up the steps.

Colin held the door open for them. "Thanks," one of the men said.

"No problem," Colin replied.

He stepped out and closed the door after him, walked quietly and calmly down the steps, then turned right and ran.

Colin didn't even know which direction he should be heading.

Earlier, he'd studied a map of the southeastern United States that Trish had given him. Between Jacksonville in Florida and Richmond in Virginia there were dozens of other cities. Colin knew that he had to go north, but which way *was* north?

When he neared the end of the block, he stopped running and ducked into a quiet shop doorway.

OK, he said to himself. *Think! Back at the shelter, at four in the afternoon, the sunlight had been coming in directly through the large window at the end of the corridor. The window was at the back of the building. This meant that the back of the building faces west and the front faces east. So I left through the front door and turned right, going south.*

I'm going in the wrong direction.

He didn't want to risk going past the front door again, so he decided to go around the block instead. He turned right at the next corner, darted quickly down an unsettlingly dark and quiet narrow street and turned right again.

And found himself facing a gang of teenagers who were gathered around a large, battered car. There were about ten of them, all in their late teens.

One of the teenagers stepped out to block Colin's path. "Well, look who it ain't!" Colin recognized him as one of Razor's gang from the shelter.

The other teenagers surrounded Colin. "*That's* him?" one of them said, his rough voice filled with disbelief. "*That's* the kid who nearly broke Razor's hand? He's a shrimp!"

Colin swallowed.

Someone got out of the car and pushed through the gang. Colin saw that it was Razor, a crazed glint in his eyes. "That kid's a lot stronger than he looks," Razor said.

A couple of the others laughed. "Oh, sure! He's a power-house, all right!"

Razor looked down at Colin. "Well, new boy. Don't feel so brave now, do you?"

"Mostly I feel tired," Colin said.

Razor laughed. "See what I was telling you? He's got a smart mouth."

I'm not going to get out of this, Colin thought. *Might as well try to minimize the damage.*

He pointed to the car. "That your car, Razor?"

"It is now."

Colin gave it an approving look. "Not bad. You're not heading north, by any chance, are you? I need to get to Richmond."

"What, Richmond in *Virginia*?"

"Yes."

Razor grinned. "Sure . . . Hop in."

When Colin hesitated, Razor grabbed him by the arm and dragged him over to the car. "Let's go for a little ride, new boy."

"On second thought, I don't think I will. But thanks."

"Now you've insulted me again."

"You're easily insulted," Colin said. He wished he hadn't.

Razor pulled the canvas bag from Colin's hand. "What's this? You a *thief,* new boy? You steal this food from the shelter?" He tossed the bag to one of his friends. "Rico, bring that stuff back before they realize it's missing." To Colin, he said, "Whenever food goes missing they always blame me. You trying to get me in trouble?"

"No, I just—"

"Put him in the car."

Two of Razor's gang took hold of him and forced him into the backseat of the car, one sitting on either side of him. Razor got into the driver's seat, revved the engine and pulled out into the street, then spun the wheel and made a quick U-turn, then turned left back up the dark street.

"I wouldn't go this way if I were you," Colin said. "Police."

The teenager on Colin's left said, "What kind of crap are you talking, new boy?"

"Trust me."

At the junction, Razor slowed the car down to a crawl. "He's right. There's a cop car pulling up outside the shelter."

Colin could see Façade's two men standing next to their own car, one of them speaking into his phone. The other one was looking around, holding one of the photographs Trish had taken.

Razor stopped the car. "Who the hell are *they*?"

Façade's agent stared in their direction, nudged his companion and showed him the photo. Colin heard him say, "That's him!"

He's spotted me! Colin realized. "Drive!" he shouted.

"Who *are* they?"

"ATF," Colin said, remembering one of the groups Trish had mentioned earlier. He wasn't sure what it meant, but it had the right effect; Razor swore, put the car into drive and roared out of the narrow street.

Colin watched as Façade's men ran back to their car. "These guys are good," he said. "You're going to have a tough time losing them."

"Oh yeah? Watch *this*—!" Razor floored the accelerator and the car sped up a tiny amount. Through the rearview mirror he could see the other car approaching fast. "What the hell have they got under the hood?"

The teenager on Colin's right said, "How do they *know*? Someone must have talked! Razor, I told you we should've dumped the booze!"

"Shut up, Ritchie!" Razor said. "OK, new boy. You're so smart, you tell me which way to go."

Colin listened. Over the roar of the engines, he could barely make out the voices of Façade's men. "They're calling for backup . . . It'll take a few minutes . . . They're reading out the license number."

"Doesn't matter," Razor said. "It's a false plate."

"So? They're going to be looking for a car with this license number. It doesn't make any difference whether it's real or not."

"Good point. All right, what next?"

"We're going south now . . . They're asking for a roadblock in . . ." Colin tried to remember the map. "St. Augustine. We need to change direction without them knowing about it."

Razor ran a red light. "And how do we do that?"

"We need to switch cars . . . Find a quiet spot, you and me will get out. Your friends here can keep driving. They're only after you," Colin lied.

Razor glanced in the rearview mirror. "It's OK. We've lost them."

He slowed the car.

Colin listened. "No, they're still coming! They took a side road . . . They're coming up on the left."

Razor did a hand brake turn and sped back up the street. "How the hell do you know all this?"

"If we get away, I'll tell you . . . OK . . . They can't see us. Pull over and stop the car somewhere dark."

"You better be right about this," Razor said.

"Trust me. I don't want to get caught any more than you do."

Razor stopped the car at a spot where the streetlights were broken and shut off the headlights.

"Here they come," Colin said. "Everyone duck down."

A few seconds later, the car with Façade's men screamed past.

Colin relaxed. "OK. They didn't see us. But they're slowing down; they know we're around here somewhere. We need to get out of here."

"All right." Razor turned to his friends and handed the car keys to the one on Colin's right. "We're swapping rides, Ritchie. Give me your keys."

Reluctantly, the boy handed his own car keys to Razor. "Don't scratch it."

"Where's it parked?"

"My mom's old apartment."

"Good. Gas?"

"I put twenty bucks in yesterday."

"Anything I need to know about it? Got anything stored in the trunk that's going to get me arrested?"

"No, nothing. Jeez, Razor! You leave the state and you're really gonna be screwed!"

"I know." He looked at Colin. "But I got my early-warning system here."

"Why can't you leave the state?" Colin asked. He was in the passenger seat of Ritchie's car. Razor was driving just under the speed limit, in a manner he hoped wouldn't attract too much attention.

"None of your damn business," Razor said. "You tell *me* something. How'd you know those guys were looking for me? How did you know which way they were going?"

Colin had been expecting this question. "I'm not sure. Sometimes I just *know* things."

"You're telling me you're psychic?"

"I don't know about that. It comes and goes."

"And how'd you do that thing with your hand?"

"It's just a matter of knowing where the pressure points are," Colin lied.

"Where'd you learn it?"

"My parents."

"What are they? Karate experts or something?"

"Something like that."

"What else can you do?"

"Not much."

Razor shook his head. "You're one weird little kid, you know that? So why do you want to get to Richmond?"

"There's an old friend of my parents' there. I'm hoping he'll be able to help me."

"That so?"

Colin nodded. "Yeah. My dad says he's very rich. He used to be an inventor."

"*How* rich?"

"Rich enough to give you a reward for helping me."

"What sort of a reward?"

"Whatever you want," Colin lied. "A new car. A new house, maybe. He's also got a lot of connections. He could get your record cleared. Give you a new identity. Like I said, whatever you want."

Razor laughed. "How about a date with Avril Lavigne?"

"Funny you should say that . . . Apparently he used to go to school with her mother's cousin. Still keeps in touch."

As Razor mulled over this very attractive idea, the car crossed over the border from Florida into Georgia.

21

DANNY COOPER WOKE UP TO FIND THAT he was half-naked and strapped to a table in a large white room. Around him, half a dozen men and women in doctors' coats were working on electronic instruments.

One of them looked at Danny. "Rachel? He's awake."

The young woman walked over to the table. "Impossible! He should be out for another three hours!"

The last thing Danny could remember was being escorted from the Lear jet into the car, when a soldier wearing medical insignia had pushed a needle into his arm.

"They must have screwed up the dose," Rachel said. She took out a penlight and shone it in Danny's eyes.

"Who are you? What is this place?"

"My name's Rachel."

"What are you doing to me?" Danny asked.

"Just a routine checkup. How are you feeling?"

"Like I want to go home."

"You'll be home soon enough."

"You're lying."

Rachel shrugged. "Any dizziness? Nausea?"

"No." Danny strained against the straps holding him down. "Let me out of here!"

"I'm afraid I can't do that. Orders, you understand."

"Who's giving the orders?"

"We've been told that you displayed an incredible burst of

speed a couple of days ago. Was that the first time such a thing has happened?"

"I'm not answering any of your questions, unless you answer mine."

"All right. But I should warn you that I don't know all the answers."

"Who's in charge here?"

"I don't think you should be concerned about that. Any prior indications that you have enhanced speed?"

"No. That was the first time. Where are we?"

"I'm not allowed to answer. Have you displayed any other unusual abilities?"

"Yes," Danny said. "I can cause anything within a hundred meters to spontaneously combust. Want a demonstration?"

Everyone in the room backed away from the table, then a voice came out of nowhere: "He's lying, Rachel."

Danny looked around to see a speaker set above a large mirror. *That has to be one-way glass,* he said to himself. *Someone's watching this.*

Rachel smiled and stepped back to the table. "Very funny. Has your friend . . ." She checked a clipboard. "Colin. Has he shown any signs of unusual abilities?"

"No. Why? What has any of this got to do with him?"

Rachel ignored the question and flipped through a couple of pages on her clipboard. "Well, he's a little younger than you. Could be another year or two before his abilities begin to manifest."

"You're saying that one of Colin's parents was a super-human too?"

She nodded. "Yes. Now that you're awake, we want to check your visual and aural acuity."

"What?"

"Your sight and hearing." She reached down beside the table and flipped a switch, and the table rotated about its center until Danny was almost upright, with only the straps keeping him from sliding off. "Now, look toward the chart, please, and read the third line."

Danny looked at the eye chart, which was pinned up on the wall about five meters away. "The third line? S. C. R. E. W. Y. O. U."

Rachel squinted at the chart. "No, that's not right." She paused. "Ah. Very funny. So, you're not going to be cooperative?"

"Would *you* be?"

Rachel reached into the pocket of her white coat and took out a small device, about half the size of a pen. She pressed it against Danny's shoulder.

Danny gasped as a powerful electric shock coursed through his entire body.

"Now," Rachel said. "The third line on the chart. Please."

This time, Danny spelled out a much ruder phrase and was shocked again.

Victor Cross and Façade watched from behind the one-way mirror. "Impressive," Victor said. "But not very productive."

"He's not going to break easily. Especially since he knows that Colin is still free."

Behind them, the door opened and Rachel entered.

"Who wants him to break?" Façade asked. "I thought you wanted him to cooperate."

Rachel said, "I really don't think that he *will* cooperate. He's too stubborn. We might have better luck with the girl."

"What's the deal with her?" Façade asked. "Who *is* she? Where did she come from?"

"Her name's Diamond," Victor said. "And she's been here all along. She can put herself in an immovable, invulnerable state. She was like that when Ragnarök's power-damper was used. She just stayed that way. We thought it was permanent."

"So how come she's back now?"

Rachel said, "There was a power surge yesterday when the nucleus was being tested. That must have triggered something."

Façade thought about this. "So if you have her, you don't need Danny, right? You can do all your tests and calibrations and whatever on her?"

Victor slowly turned to look at him. "You need an extra pair of socks, Façade?"

"What?"

"Sounds to me like you're getting cold feet."

"Don't push me, Cross! I'm as committed to this as anyone! I gave up eleven years of my life for this!"

Rachel said, "If you two are done seeing who can spit the farthest? We still have a situation to deal with. We need Danny's cooperation. I don't think that forcing him or threatening him is the right way to go. I think we need to send in Joseph. Right now, he's explaining everything to the Wagners. Or trying to, at least. He's still a little confused."

Danny heard someone enter the room and opened his eyes to see Façade standing in front of him.

"You're going to have to cooperate, Danny," Façade said.

Danny raised his head a little, looked down at the bruises and scorch marks on his arms. "They're torturing me and you're letting them do it!"

Façade bit his lip. "All they want to do is figure out the extent of your powers."

"Why? What do they need to know that for?"

"I can't tell you that. Do what they say and everything will turn out fine. Trust me."

"Trust you? *Trust* you? You pretended to be my father for the past eleven years! I don't even know what happened to my *real* father! I don't know whether he's alive or dead."

"Danny, I'm sorry about having to pretend that I was your father, but it was necessary." He paused. "And . . . I know you won't want to believe this, but it was *his* idea."

"Whose?"

Façade walked over to the door, opened it and left.

Seconds later, a tall, thin bearded man walked into the room. His skin was pale, lined with age.

Danny watched as the man approached the table and smiled nervously at him. "Hello, son."

22

DANNY WATCHED AS THE THIN MAN dragged a chair over to the table and sat down.

"Aren't you going to say hello?" the man asked.

"Who *are* you?"

"I'm your father."

Danny swallowed. "You're . . ." He stared at him. There was definitely a strong resemblance between this man and Façade.

"I can only guess how you must be feeling. I'd be surprised too. I don't expect you to call me Dad. You can call me by my middle name—Joseph."

"What . . . What's this about?"

"It's about a prophecy . . . Danny, there were times when I could see the future. Not always. I couldn't control that ability. In fact, usually when it happened I couldn't actually *see* the future, but I got a sense of it. Do you know what I mean?"

Danny shook his head. "It's not possible."

"Oh, it was possible. It's just not something I could control."

"That's not what I'm talking about. It's not possible that you're really my father."

"I promise you, it's true."

"And you were Quantum?"

"That's right."

"But you were one of the good guys."

"I still am, Danny."

"You're working *with* these people! For God's sake! Can't you see that they're evil? They kidnapped me and Colin and his parents!"

"They're not evil, Danny. Look, you don't know the whole story."

"Then tell me. What is this all about?"

Joseph smiled. "It's all about you, Danny. Right from day one, it's *always* been all about you."

Danny tried to roll away, to get off the table, but the straps were holding him tight. "If you are my father, then get me out of here!"

"I can't do that, Danny."

"Then tell me what's going on! Why did you let Façade replace you?"

"He was the only one who could do it. If Titan and the others had figured out what we were planning, they'd have tried to stop us. The only way we could succeed was for Façade to take my place. He . . ." Joseph smiled. "He took some persuading, but in the end we found out what Façade wanted and we were able to offer that to him."

"What was it?"

"A chance to stop running, to have a normal life. A lot of superhumans never used their powers, did you know that? We don't know how many of us there were—hundreds, maybe—and some of them chose not to become superheroes. It's not natural, you see. That's what we realized. The powers were—*are*—something we were never meant to have. The human race isn't ready for that sort of responsibility."

"But that's like . . . like not letting *anyone* drive a car just because a couple of people are dangerous behind the wheel! You can't just *decide* to take everyone's powers away!"

"Yes. We can and we did. But not just for that reason. No one knew for sure how the powers worked," Joseph said. "Where did they come from? Why did some people develop powers and others didn't? The only one who had any kind of grasp of it was Ragnarök. We knew that because he'd once learned how to temporarily boost his own strength. *How* he did that, we were never sure."

Danny said, "You keep saying 'we.' Who else was involved?"

"Do you want me to tell you this story or not?"

"Go on."

Joseph started to speak, then frowned. "Where was I?"

"Ragnarök."

"Right. We had to remove everyone's powers. That way everyone would be safe. But the only way to do that was to work with Ragnarök. He was smart, you see. A genius. But completely mad. The point is, Ragnarök was the only one who could build the power-damper. He thought that the machine would take away every other superhuman's powers and then—at some stage in the future—he'd be able to reabsorb that power himself."

"But . . . why didn't Ragnarök just use the machine? Why did he build the battle-tank?"

"Because the power-damper works by stripping the superhuman energy and absorbing it back into itself. But the amount of power it absorbs is relative to the distance. The closer a superhuman is to the machine, the more of their power it will take."

"So he built something big enough and dangerous enough that it would bring every superhero running?"

Joseph nodded. "And not just the heroes. He wanted the villains' power as well. He recruited everyone he could think of. He didn't know that we knew what he was up to, though. He'd designed a force field to protect himself from the effects of the power-damper, but I'd sabotaged it. It would never have worked. Titan breaching the force field didn't make any difference from that point of view."

"And while you were working with Ragnarök . . ."

"Façade took my place. Exactly. Façade was the best choice—the only choice—to take my place and look after you."

"So what does this have to do with me?" Danny asked. "I was only four years old then!"

"We hadn't anticipated that Titan would do so much damage to the battle-tank. The tank exploded seconds after the power-damper was activated. The machine was destroyed and we had no way to build another one. We'd intended to keep it active forever, to strip your powers when they manifested."

"But *why*?"

"Because the day you were born," Joseph said, "well, it was the best day of my life. And the worst day. It was the day of the prophecy."

"What do you mean?"

"You were only a few minutes old when I held you in my arms for the first time. I saw something then. I saw the future. The vision was clearer than any I'd had before. It . . . Danny, I saw what you would become. I saw an army gathering on the horizon; hate in their eyes; blood on their hands; death in their hearts. And leading them was you. My son." He closed his eyes. "I can't touch the future anymore, Danny, but I can remember what I saw then. I saw the day coming when all the world's heroes will stand against you and be destroyed. There will be no one left to protect the world. In your hatred and anger, you will lay waste to the Earth."

Joseph opened his eyes and stared at Danny. "Billions of innocent people will die."

Danny shook his head. "No! No, that's not true! That won't happen!"

"It *will* happen, *if* we don't strip you of your superhuman powers. You said that these people here are evil. You're wrong, Danny. They're not evil. They're trying to save the world— they're trying to save it from you."

23

VICTOR CROSS SANG QUIETLY TO HIM-
self as he strode along the dusty corridor, a mug of coffee in one
hand, a palmtop computer in the other. A trio of passing soldiers
gave him an odd glance, but Victor ignored them.

Victor's multitasking mind was working overtime.

As he walked, he was mentally assembling the power-
damping machine, deciding what his next move with Joseph
would be, wondering what to do about Diamond, calculating
the compound interest his savings would earn if he moved them
to a high-yield account and working out the next ten moves in
the thirty-one games of chess he'd been playing over the Internet
for the past three weeks.

Victor stopped outside a guarded room, showed his pass-card
to the guards and unlocked the door.

Inside, four white-coated technicians, two men and two
women, were assembling and testing various electronic and mechanical components. Huge blueprints were pinned all around
the walls and one of the technicians was examining one of these
very closely.

"Problems?" Victor asked, looking at the blueprint.

"Nothing we can't handle, Mr. Cross."

Victor sipped at his coffee. "Now, that's not true, is it, Mr.
Laurie? You're lost in a sea of cables and components. You want
to tell me where you're stuck?"

Laurie turned toward one of the workbenches. "We're having trouble with the miniaturization. Ragnarök's force field generator was the size of a Buick. We've been able to get it down to this." He pointed to a piece of equipment that was a little larger than a backpack.

"That's not good enough."

"I know. We haven't been able to get it any smaller."

"It works?"

"I think so, yes. Look, if the others found out what we were doing . . ."

"Don't worry about what *they* might do," Victor said. "Worry about what *I'll* do if you let me down."

Laurie swallowed. "Look, we don't know how to reduce it any further. I'm sorry, but this is as small as it gets. It will work, though. It'll shield anyone within a four-meter radius from the effects of the power-damper."

"No. It needs to be much, much smaller than this, and it has to run continuously. Our benefactor can *not* afford to lose his abilities. Either we perfect this shield, or we sabotage the power-damper. Which is not going to be easy, because since the null-field went online it's practically invulnerable."

"It might help if we knew more about how the power-damper works . . ." Laurie glanced at Victor. "I know you don't want us to know too much about it, but the more we know the easier this will be."

Victor thought about this. "All right. Everyone? Attention, please!"

The other technicians stopped what they were doing and looked up.

"The power-damper works by stripping the superhuman energies, right?"

They nodded.

"No, wrong," Victor said. "Ragnarök was able to build *his* machine because he understood what the powers are and how they work. And more important, why only some people are affected by them. The truth is that it's not just a power-damper. It's a siphon, a capacitor. It strips the energy from the superhumans and draws that energy into itself." He smiled. "Beginning to understand? Yes?"

Victor sighed when he saw their blank expressions. "You people are supposed to be the best physicists on the planet! Laurie, tell us about the conservation of energy."

"It's the principle that the sum of the total amount of energy and mass in an isolated system will always be constant."

"Which means?"

"It means that if you remove energy from something, the energy doesn't just disappear. It has to go somewhere."

"Right. The power-damper strips and it stores. Ragnarök built it that way—but he wanted to steal the other superhumans' energy and then find a way to use it himself." Victor paused. "He never got a chance to work out how to do that, but the machine itself was sound. It *did* strip all the superhumans' powers."

"How strong does the force field need to be?" the other male technician asked.

"The key is not the *strength* of the field; it's the frequency. It has to operate at exactly thirty-two point seven-five-four femtohertz."

One of the women said, "I think we can do it. We can make a miniature force field generator that will operate permanently at the right frequency. It'll be ready before the power-damper is, and it'll be undetectable."

Victor grinned. "Now, *that's* what I want to hear! Excellent! I couldn't be more proud."

Laurie said, "Mr. Cross . . . wouldn't it just be simpler to sabotage the power-damper? Then your benefactor wouldn't lose his powers."

"And neither would Danny Cooper or any of the new heroes. You don't understand. Our benefactor wants to be the *only* superhuman. And more than that . . . It *is* possible for the superhuman powers to be reabsorbed by someone else. Ragnarök just couldn't figure out how to make it work. He wasn't smart enough. I am."

24

Colin jumped. "What? What is it?" He rubbed his eyes and looked out through the windscreen. He could see nothing but a trail of streetlights fading off into the night. The driver's side window was open and the warm breeze was flicking Razor's long hair around his face. "Where are we?"

"Just passed Sumter, South Carolina. We're about halfway, but we're running low on gas. You got any money?"

"Ten dollars."

"That's all? Damn. I've only got about five on me. Unless we can get more money for gas, we're not going to make it as far as Virginia." Razor hesitated for a second, then said, "We might have to make a withdrawal on credit." He glanced at Colin. "You get what I mean? We go for the special offer. Zero dollars down, and zero dollars to pay each month for the next eighteen months."

"You're talking about robbing a petrol station?"

"In this part of the world, we call it *gas*, not petrol. Yeah. That's what I'm talking about."

"No way," Colin said. "If you try anything like that I really *will* break your arm."

"How did I know you were going to say that?"

"What time is it?"

"Three-thirty." Razor yawned and slapped his face. "And I'm

falling asleep here. You gotta keep me awake, OK? The radio's busted, so talk to me."

"What do you want to know?"

"You can start with what's going on. Why are you running away?"

"You want the whole story? The truth?"

"Yeah. And pass me another Coke." He jerked his thumb toward the backseat, where Colin saw a shopping bag packed with junk food.

He handed a can to Razor, who quickly popped the tab and drained half the contents in one gulp.

"When did you get this stuff?"

"Rest stop about fifty miles back."

"What, you left me asleep in the car?"

"Yeah. Well, there was no one around for miles. You weren't in any danger. Besides, you're the one who's psychic."

"It's not like that."

"Then what *is* it like?" Razor asked. "I mean, here I am, middle of the night, on the run with a foreign kid who can read people's minds, or whatever, and you know something? I don't think those guys in Jacksonville were after *me* at all. I think they were looking for *you*. What do you say to that?"

Colin hesitated. "Razor, if I tell you the truth, I'll be putting you in danger."

"I'm already *in* danger, helping you out. I must be losing my mind. So . . . Speak. Tell me everything."

Colin decided that there was no point in hiding anything. "You won't believe me."

"Let *me* decide that."

"Ten years ago, all the superheroes attacked Ragnarök's battle-tank and then disappeared."

"This much I know. I was seven at the time. I remember it."

"OK. Well, the fact is that they *didn't* disappear. I mean they weren't killed. They just went into hiding. What happened was that Ragnarök used a weapon that stripped them of their powers. The bad guys were arrested or escaped and the heroes all returned to their normal lives."

"And how would you know this?"

"Because my father was Titan and my mother was Energy."

Razor laughed. "Oh yeah, sure!"

"It's true."

"And this Solomon Cord we're going to see, he used to be a superhero too?"

"He was Paragon."

"Why should I believe you? And you still haven't said why you're on the run."

Colin explained about Façade taking Quantum's place, about the discovery of Danny's powers and the subsequent kidnapping. Razor wasn't inclined to believe any of it.

"You know what I can do," Colin said. "My powers are only just beginning to appear. That's how I was able to know what the men chasing us were up to; I'm not psychic, I was able to *hear* them."

"And this is how you damn near crushed my hand? Superstrength?"

"I think so."

Razor shook his head and laughed. "So you're telling me that I'm sitting next to someone who's going to be one of the next generation of superhumans? We're quite a pair, aren't we? A superhuman and a car thief."

"That's what you do? Steal cars?"

"Hey, everyone's good at *something,* right? Me, I'm good at locks and engines. My old man always said, 'Find something you're good at and stick with it.'" He noticed Colin's expression, then added, "It's not like they have to pay for it themselves. They have insurance."

"You check that, do you? Before you steal someone's car, you make sure that they're covered and they won't need their car for a few days?"

Razor gave him a look of disgust. "Don't give me that crap! In this world you have to take what you can get. Maybe you grew up in a nice little house with Mommy and Daddy looking after you, giving you everything you wanted, but some people weren't so lucky."

"That doesn't excuse stealing from someone else. What about *this* car? Is it stolen too?"

"No. Ritchie's mother gave it to him. It was a wreck. It took us two months to strip and rebuild the engine."

"Then why don't you get a job fixing up cars?"

"Because it takes us a couple of minutes to boost a car, and we can get maybe three hundred bucks for it from this guy I know."

"You take the risk and he gets most of the money."

"Look, sometimes you just *do* stuff, all right?"

"OK."

"Anyway, we're getting out of the car business. It's getting too dangerous. Last month a guy we know was trying to boost this guy's car and the guy came out and shot him. Damn near blew his hand off."

"What are you going to do instead?"

"I know an old guy who makes his own homemade booze. Good stuff too. He's got a whole cellar full of it. I told him I knew a guy who'd give him ten bucks a bottle." Razor grinned. "Which is a lot less than we're *really* getting for it."

"So you're what, about seventeen? And you've already graduated from being a car thief to selling illegal alcohol. What's next? Drugs? Kidnapping? Murder?"

Razor slammed his fist against the steering wheel. "Screw you, Colin! What the hell gives *you* the right to judge me? You ungrateful little . . ."

"OK, OK. I'm sorry."

"Jeez . . . You're something else, you know that? I put myself out for you and you pay me back with insults!"

"I didn't mean it like that. I didn't mean that you *would* do any of that stuff. I'm just saying that you're, well . . ."

Razor suddenly grinned. "I'm on the slippery slope?"

"Kind of."

"Lot of guys like me end up doing serious time. That won't happen to me. The trick to surviving it is to *know* that you're on the slope and to know when to get off."

"How did you get your name?" Colin suddenly asked.

"What?"

"Why are you called Razor?"

"No reason, just a nickname."

"What's your real name?"

Razor looked at him with suspicion. "Why?"

"I'm curious."

"I'm not going to tell you my real name."

"OK. But I don't know anything about you. I mean, apart from the fact that you're a car thief and that you like picking on kids smaller than you."

"It's not like that. You have to make sure everyone knows where you stand."

"So why did you try to hurt *me*? Did I look like the sort of person who might challenge your leadership?"

"Every new kid gets checked out. Make sure they know their place."

"It sounds like you're just being a bully."

Razor suddenly laughed. "A bully! Man, you're up on all the really harsh putdowns, aren't you?"

Colin grinned. Razor seemed wide awake now, less likely to nod off at the wheel.

Shortly after four in the morning, Razor steered the car off the freeway and stopped at a huge neon-lit gas station. They pooled their money. "All right . . . We got sixteen bucks and change. Way this thing eats gas, that might just get us to the next town, but not much farther."

"Where will that leave us?"

"About a hundred and twenty miles short of Richmond. Plus we gotta stop somewhere, get some sleep. Unless you can drive?"

"No, sorry," Colin said.

Razor looked around. There were four other cars parked nearby. "No good . . ."

"You're not thinking about stealing another car, are you?"

"No. It'd be reported and we wouldn't get more than ten miles. No, I was hoping for a camper or something. They usually have reserve gas tanks."

"I don't want to steal from someone."

Razor sighed. "Colin, what's worse? We steal fifty bucks' worth of gas from someone or we never get to Richmond, which means we won't be able to find your folks' friend?"

"It doesn't feel right. Don't you have a credit card or something?"

"I don't even have an address. Sure, American Express is just dying to give *me* a credit card."

"Well, is there anything we can sell?"

"No . . . but I have an idea."

Colin rushed into the gas station's diner and shouted, "There's a white Toyota on fire out there!"

There was a brief pause as everyone turned to look at him, then a middle-aged man said, "That's *my* car!" and charged out.

Colin ran after him, just in time to watch Razor using his jacket to beat out the flames from the rear of the man's car.

"Stay back!" Razor said. "I think it's out, but we'd better give it a coupla minutes." He turned to the man and said, "We were on the way in and there was this sort of 'whoof' sound and I saw these flames."

"Hell," the man said. "Better call the fire department."

"No, I don't think it's serious," Razor said.

The man looked around and said, to no one in particular,

"Listen to this! My car was on fire and he doesn't think it's serious!"

"You just filled up the tank, right?"

"That's right."

"And you've been driving all night, yeah? Probably just some gas splashed out, ignited on the tailpipe. A coupla more minutes and it woulda been a fireball."

The man gave Razor a friendly slap on the back. "Thanks, kid. Good going."

A stick-thin, middle-aged woman came out. "Everything OK?"

"This boy here's just saved our car," the man said. "Saw the flames and put the fire out."

"It's no trouble," Razor said. "Just glad I could help."

The man turned to Colin. "Your brother is a very brave young man."

Colin beamed proudly. "I know. He's been looking after me since Mom got sick."

The woman put her arm around him. "Oh, you poor boy!" She turned to her husband. "Give them something, Bernie."

The man reached into the pocket of his slacks, but Razor backed away. "No, thanks! We don't take charity from anyone." He headed back toward his own car.

"Sorry, mister," Colin said. "After my dad left, Wayne promised Mom that he'd take care of all of us."

They watched as Razor drove his car up to the gas pumps.

Colin remembered a line from an old cowboy movie. "He says a man's pride is all he has at the end of the day."

"Where are you boys headed at this hour?" the woman asked.

"Orlando. We're going to try and find our dad, get him to pay all the alimony he owes. We heard he lives there now."

"Your accent is a little unusual," the man said. "Where are you from?"

"Pennsylvania, originally," Colin said. "But I was living with Mom's sister in Scotland until a few years ago. They sent me home because . . . well, like I said, my mom's not well and . . ." He trailed off, and tried to look like he was struggling to hold back tears.

The man patted him on the shoulder. "It'll be OK," he said. He looked over at Razor, who was filling the tank and was very obviously trying not to put in more than sixteen dollars' worth. "Your brother's a good man. He'll take care of you." He lowered his voice. "Look, there's nothing wrong with a man having his pride. But he shouldn't be *too* proud, you know what I mean?"

"No," Colin lied.

The man took out his wallet and pressed some money into Colin's hand. "You can tell him about this when you're on the road and it's too late for him to refuse, OK?"

Colin felt wracked with guilt at his deception, and this must have shown up on his face.

"Take it," the woman said.

"We don't deserve this."

"It's a reward."

"We *really* don't deserve it," Colin said. To himself he added, *At least* that *bit is true.*

"Then consider it a gift."

"Thank you. It'll make a big difference."

The man patted him on the shoulder again. "You look after your mom and Wayne, all right?"

"I will. Thanks again." He held his hand out to the man. "My name's Bernard, by the way."

"No kidding? That's my name too!"

"How much did we get?" Razor asked as soon as they reached the freeway.

Colin counted the money. "Five twenties and a fifty. A hundred and fifty dollars."

Razor laughed. "Man, that was great!"

"It was wrong."

"Colin, you saw the way they were dressed, you saw the size of their car. Those people are rich. A hundred and fifty bucks is *nothing* to them. And look what they got for their money: they now believe that they've helped some less well-off folks. They're gonna be feeling good about this for weeks. That's gotta be worth a hundred and fifty bucks."

Colin wasn't sure. "Maybe."

"Trust me. Nice touch pretending you had the same name as that guy, by the way. You're a natural grifter."

"I don't like the sound of that."

Razor laughed again. "Look, now we've got enough money to get to Richmond and find your friend. What are you complaining about?"

"We shouldn't have done it."

"You're telling me that you didn't enjoy that? Colin, you just ripped off two sweet old folks and you did it better than I would have. You remember that, next time you start thinking you've got the moral high ground."

"Look, I didn't have a choice! I have to get to Solomon Cord!"

"So the ends justify the means, yeah?"

Colin said nothing. He knew that what he had done was wrong, but he also knew that Razor was right.

Colin had enjoyed it, and that scared him.

25

DANNY COOPER STOOD IN THE EXAMI-
nation room, stripped to the waist, as Rachel stuck dozens of
small white plastic dots to his chest.

Rachel said, "Your muscles seem underdeveloped for a boy
of your age. Do you exercise much?"

Danny ignored her. He had refused to speak since the conversation with his father.

"How's your metabolism?" she asked. "Are you eating regu-
larly?"

Not since I got here, Danny thought to himself.

Rachel didn't seem bothered that Danny was ignoring her.
She checked some of the plastic dots, ticking them off on a list
attached to her clipboard.

"OK, Danny. That machine over there scans these markers
and logs their position. When you move, we can track the stress
on your muscles. Unfortunately, the scanner can't track enough
markers for us to do your whole body in one go, so we'll have
to do your legs later. We should be able to match up the data
easily enough."

When Rachel turned to key information into her computer,
Danny switched some of the markers around.

The woman didn't seem to notice. "This is very similar to
the system that movie people use when they want to do motion
capture. You know what that is? They track an actor's move-
ments and afterward the computer can reproduce those move-

ments exactly. OK . . . Now to start with, I just want you to walk around."

Danny didn't move.

Rachel sighed and took the electric shock device out of her pocket. "You want me to use this again?"

Go ahead, Danny thought. *I hope it interferes with your instruments. I should be able to get out of here anyway. OK, so my powers aren't exactly reliable, but I'm still the only one here who* has *any sort of powers. If I can move as fast as I did when that bus was coming for Susie, they'll never be able to stop me.*

But getting past the heavy door, and the two soldiers standing guard on either side of it, was going to be a problem. The door hadn't been opened since shortly after his father had left.

Danny still couldn't believe what Joseph had told him. *He had a vision of me fourteen years ago, and because of that he ruined my whole life.*

Rachel was asking him something, but Danny wasn't paying attention.

Then, he suddenly sensed that she was pushing the shocker toward the small of his back.

Danny spun around and knocked the device out of her hand.

Rachel stared at him. "How did . . . ? My God!" She turned to one of the technicians. "Did you get that? Tell me you got that!"

"I got it! Correlating the data now!"

The technician's screen cleared to show a series of dots. Rachel said to Danny, "Have a look at this!"

Curiosity got the better of Danny, and he followed her to the computer station.

The technician clicked on a button marked "Replay," and Danny saw the dots blur for a second.

"Link the markers so we can see it more clearly," Rachel said to him. "By the way, Danny, it makes no difference that you moved some of the markers. Nice try, though."

On screen, the series of dots turned into a network of lines, roughly forming the shape of a man's chest and arms. "That's you standing still," Rachel explained. "See how it swells and ebbs? That's your chest as you breathe."

As Danny watched, the figure on the screen was suddenly facing the other way, one of its arms outstretched.

Rachel asked, "What's the time resolution?"

The technician switched to a different screen and flipped through page after page of numbers. "We're getting one thousand and twenty-four readings a second. That's optimal."

"All right. Show me the sequence again, but this time, I want to see it played back in real time, not speeded up."

"Rachel, that *was* real time. He really spun around that fast."

"Good Lord . . . Replay at one-tenth speed."

Even slowed down, the figure on screen spun around faster than the eye could track.

"Skip to just before the turn, then run it one frame a second," Rachel said.

The technician tapped at the keyboard for a few seconds. "OK . . ."

On screen, the figure seemed to be completely still, then its muscles tensed and it turned around, lashing its hand out at the same time. The process took ten frames.

"Amazing! In real time, that's less than a hundredth of a second," Rachel said. "We need to do that again, see how his feet move. Danny, strip down to your shorts."

For the first time in hours, Danny spoke. "No."

"We've *never* had the chance to examine a superhuman before, Danny. This equipment wasn't even invented ten years ago. We want to see everything that you can do."

Again, Danny said, "No."

"We have to know how fast you are."

Danny held up his right hand and opened it. "Fast enough to pick this up without you even noticing I'd moved." In his hand, he held Rachel's shocking device.

He pressed it against her neck and pushed the button.

Rachel yelped and stumbled back.

"Hurts, doesn't it?"

One of the soldiers at the door pulled out his gun and aimed at Danny . . . who was no longer there.

The soldier barely had time to say, "Where—?" before he too was shocked in the neck. Before the man could even react, Danny had shocked his companion, taken their keys and unlocked the door.

On the other side of the one-way glass, Victor Cross glanced at the device on his wrist. It looked like an ordinary wristwatch.

It wasn't.

Danny ran through the dark mine shafts, easily dodging the many guards and workers, who seemed to be almost frozen in place.

He had no idea which way he was going, but he wasn't bothered about that: he was moving so fast that he was sure he'd find the exit before anyone could catch him. The only problem was that the faster he moved, the darker the tunnels became.

In a small cavern, he stopped to watch two workers who were attempting to fix a leaking water pipe.

The men moved in a plodding slow motion, as did the spray of water. Danny saw one drop of water arc toward him so slowly that he was easily able to step aside and watch as it smoothly and silently splashed against the ground, raising a small cloud of dust.

It's like I've altered my perception of time, Danny said to himself. *This isn't just me running faster; I'm* living *faster.*

As an experiment, he picked up a fist-sized rock and let it drop from shoulder height. To his perception, the rock took over twenty seconds to hit the ground.

He picked up the rock again and threw it as hard as he could against the far wall; the rock seemed to move at what was, to him, a fairly normal speed, but when it hit the wall it shattered, silently, as though it had been a ball of dried mud.

At this speed, he realized, he couldn't hear anything. The sound waves were too slow for his ears to register.

But the two workers *did* hear it. Danny watched, fascinated, as the men reacted to the sound; slowly, methodically, they turned toward where the rock had hit.

Amazing! Danny thought. *I could do* anything!

He walked over to the nearest man, and stepped right in front of him. *Can he even* see *me?* Danny wondered.

From the way the man's expression changed, the way his eyes

widened before settling on him, it was clear that he could be seen if he stayed still long enough.

So I'm not invisible. Pity.

He left the cavern and returned to the maze of tunnels, running at what felt like a gentle pace, but still much faster than anyone could react.

He found himself back on the corridor that led to the examination room and saw that Façade was running—with glacial slowness—toward the room.

Danny zipped past him, turned left and found himself at the end of a very long, wide corridor that sloped upward. There were dusty tire tracks on the ground.

This has to be the way out.

He raced up the corridor. It ended in a large cavern in which dozens of men, most of them armed, were unloading equipment from huge army trucks. At the far side of the cavern were two huge reinforced metal doors.

The doors were closed and clearly locked; three steel bars, each at least twenty centimeters thick, had been slid in place across them.

There's got to be another way out.

He turned back and began to explore the mine.

Everywhere he went, he saw soldiers carrying equipment, standing on guard, escorting other people. All of them were standing still or frozen in midstride.

The light is definitely getting darker the faster I go . . . Strange.

Façade burst into the examination room, where he saw the two guards helping Rachel to her feet.

"What the hell happened here?"

"He just disappeared," Rachel said. "His power . . . My God, I've never seen anything like it!"

"How long will it last?"

Rachel shrugged. "It's impossible to say."

"He could be a thousand miles away by now," Façade said.

She shook her head. "No, the entrance is sealed. There's no way out without a pass code."

"Won't the power-damper work wherever he is?" Façade asked.

"I don't think we should take that chance; we can't be certain that our machine will work as well as Ragnarök's did. I say we seal off the unused tunnels and reduce the number of places for him to hide."

A voice behind them said, "I say we let him go."

Rachel and Façade turned to see Victor Cross and Joseph standing in the doorway. "Let him go," Victor repeated. "If we keep him trapped here, he might damage something."

"We need him, Victor," Rachel said. "We didn't get enough data to properly calibrate the power-damper!"

"We *don't* need him," Victor said. "We have the girl. She's a superhuman, so she's viable. Plus she's a lot more stable than Danny is. Rachel, tell the guards to open the main door."

Rachel unclipped her communicator from her belt, hit the activation button and began to speak into it.

The communicator disappeared.

Rachel stared at her empty hand. "What—?" She turned to Victor. "Did you see that?"

Victor was staring over Rachel's shoulder.

She turned to see Danny Cooper standing in the doorway. In one hand, he had Rachel's communicator. In the other, he was holding one of the guards' guns.

26

THERE IS NO WAY OUT OF THIS, RENATA said to herself.

She was being kept in a large, empty room, somewhere on one of the mine's upper levels.

The guard at the door had his gun trained on her at all times.

Renata was sitting on an uncomfortable metal chair, the only thing in the room. They'd tried to handcuff her three times, and each time she'd snapped through the cuffs.

"Can I get something to eat?" she asked.

"No."

"Please?"

"I said no."

From far below, Renata could hear a siren. "What's that?"

Without taking his eyes off her, the guard spoke into his walkie-talkie. "This is Escher on level one. What's going on?"

A voice crackled in reply: "Maintain your position, Escher. We've had a security breach. We're handling it."

"Roger."

"Look, you can't just let me *starve* to death!" Renata tried again.

"That's not up to me."

"Then at least tell me what's going on here."

"No. Now shut up."

"You don't know, do you?" She risked a smile. "You have no idea who I am and what I can do!"

"I know you can turn yourself into some weird hard substance and that you're very strong. I also know that your strength isn't any good to you right now, because I could shoot you down before you got anywhere near me."

"But—"

He interrupted her. "And I know that when you're invulnerable you can't move. So whichever way you look at it, you're trapped here. You might as well get used to the idea."

The guard's walkie-talkie crackled again. "Escher? This is Davison. What's your status?"

"No change, sir."

"Good. We have a problem here. Seems the kid has got Cross and the others hostage. You sit tight until you're called, got that?"

"Sir."

Renata said, "Looks like you're stuck here too. So who's the boy?"

"I don't know. And you don't need to know."

"Are they, like, *paying* you for this? I mean, I know that this isn't a military operation, despite what it looks like. So they're paying you, right? I hope it's worth it. I hope that you can sleep at night, knowing that you're working for the bad guys."

"What makes you think that we're the bad guys? All we've done is taken a few civilians in for questioning. That's acceptable, when you consider that the security of the world is at stake."

"And is it?"

"From what I'm told, yes."

"You believe them? Then you're a fool. The good guys don't take innocent people hostage. The good guys don't have some sort of doomsday machine in the basement."

The guard laughed. "That's not a doomsday machine, kid. That's salvation."

She smiled. "Oh, sure."

At least he's talkative. If I can get him to relax, to lower his gun a little, then I might have a chance.

She'd calculated that she would need about a second. Any less than that and the guard would have enough time to pull the trigger.

Renata was willing to wait, even if it took hours.

After ten years, what difference would another couple of hours make?

27

RAZOR SHOOK HIMSELF AWAKE SUDDENLY.
What was I dreaming about? he wondered. *Oh yeah, I was dreaming that I'd spent the whole night driving.*

Then he realized that it hadn't been a dream and that he was still behind the wheel of the car.

And that the car was moving.

He screamed. "Oh *crap!*"

Colin jumped. He'd been half-asleep, staring out the passenger window at the dawn sun rising over an endless line of trees. "What is it?"

"Just remembered I was supposed to meet someone this morning," Razor lied. To himself, he said, *Jeez, I've got to pull over.*

"Where are we?" Colin asked. "We must be nearly there by now."

Razor had no idea where they were. He remembered passing a road sign, but couldn't recall what had been written on it. *I know we passed Raleigh. Have we reached Petersburg yet?*

"Where are we?" Colin repeated.

"Nearly there. Exactly where does this guy live?"

"Some place called Highland Springs. Do you know it?"

"Oh, sure, Colin. I know *everywhere* in America. Man, I wish the radio was working. Then we'd be able to pick up the local stations, get a feel for where we are."

"So you *don't* know?"

"Not so much. I kind of zoned out for a while there. That happens when you drive all night."

"Pull over, then. Get some rest."

"No, we're nearly there. Probably." He rolled down the window and let the cool morning air blast through the car. "Any food left?"

Colin reached around and picked up the bag of groceries. "Sure. What do you want?"

"Gimme one of those energy bars."

"Which flavor? There's banana, apple or pineapple."

"Apple."

Colin handed the bar to Razor and opened a banana one for himself. It was basically banana-flavored sugar wrapped in chocolate, with half a dozen raisins added so that the manufacturer could pass it off as health food.

"So what's your plan when we find Paragon?" Razor asked. "How's he going to help find your folks?"

"I don't know. But he's the only chance I have. Unless I can get to Max Dalton."

"But that guy never sees anyone. He's a total recluse."

"And he lives in New York, so that puts him completely out of reach. Unless you feel like driving there instead?"

Razor pretended to think about this. "No, let's just stick with the original plan."

Razor stopped the car outside the ivy-covered house. "That's it. Number 1620. You sure you remembered the address correctly?"

"Positive," Colin said, staring out at the house. They'd

reached Highland Springs half an hour earlier and had stopped at a gas station to use the bathroom and buy a map of the area.

"Then let's go. And let's hope that he's not on vacation." Razor opened the car door, got out and stretched, every joint clicking and popping.

Colin climbed out of the car, very aware of how tired and dirty he must have looked.

"Can you hear anything?" Razor asked.

Colin concentrated, but his enhanced hearing didn't seem to be working at the moment. "No."

"Only works at certain times, is that it?"

"Yeah. I'm sure that eventually I'll be able to do it whenever I want."

"We don't have time for 'eventually.'"

Taking a deep breath, Colin walked up to the front door and rang the bell.

After a minute, the steel garage door was rolled up by a large middle-aged black man wearing grease-covered overalls: the same man from the picture on Trish's computer. In the garage behind him, Colin could see that he'd been working on the engine of an old car. The engine was suspended above the car, hanging by heavy chains from a series of pulleys set into the ceiling.

He looked at Colin and Razor and raised an eyebrow. "Can I help you boys?"

"Are you Solomon Cord?" Colin asked.

"That's me. What can I do for you?" He pulled a dirty rag out of a pocket and wiped his hands on it.

"We need your help. I was sent to find you."

"That so?"

"You used to know my parents. They're in trouble."

Cord sighed. "Look, get lost, kid. I'm tired of you people always coming around looking for a handout. Last month, it was 'our car's out of gas and we just need a couple of bucks to get us back home.' Before that, it was the sick baby sister routine."

"This isn't a scam," Colin said. "I'm serious! Look . . . I know that you used to be Paragon."

Solomon Cord raised his eyes. "Get the hell out of here before I throw you out!"

"No. We've come too far. Mr. Cord, you *knew* my parents. They used to be Titan and Energy."

"Yeah, sure. And I suppose your friend here with the stupid blond hair used to be Santa Claus." He leaned closer to Colin. "Now, you listen to me, boy. You start telling people that sort of bull about me and I will track you down and use your head for a football and your rib cage for a CD rack, got that?"

Cord stepped back into the garage, reached up to the door and pulled it down. The door slammed shut.

Colin and Razor looked at each other.

"So you got the wrong man," Razor said. "Fantastic. You tricked me into driving six hundred miles and we don't have enough money to get back to Florida. Now what do we do?"

Colin gritted his teeth. "We are *not* giving up!" He clenched his fist and pounded on the garage door. "Mr. Cord!"

From inside the garage, Cord's voice shouted, "That's it! I'm calling the cops!"

Razor said, "OK, I'm out of here! Colin, you're on your own!"

He turned and walked back toward the car.

"No! Damn you, Cord!" Colin crouched down, hooked his fingers under the garage door and pulled up. The metal door screamed as the lock was ripped apart.

Colin stepped into the garage; Solomon Cord was standing at the back, behind the car, a heavy wrench in his hands.

"How the hell did you do that?"

Colin reached out and grabbed hold of the car's engine, ripping it from its chains. "I *said*, I need your help, Mr. Cord!"

He lifted the engine above his head. His muscles were taut but not strained, his face relaxed.

Cord dropped the wrench and stared. "God . . . It's true."

"Are you going to *listen* to me?"

He looked Colin up and down. "I am now."

28

COLIN LOWERED THE MASSIVE ENGINE TO the ground.

"What's your name?" Solomon Cord asked.

"Colin Wagner. My parents are Warren and Caroline. They were also known as—"

"I know who they are," Cord interrupted. He peered at Colin. "Yeah. I can kind of see a resemblance. So what sort of trouble are your folks in?"

"It's a long story. I just need to know if you're going to help me."

"Of course I will."

"My dad told me to find either you or Max Dalton. You were closest."

Solomon Cord nodded. "All right. Let's go inside."

Colin turned and saw Razor standing there, eyes wide and mouth dropped open.

Razor looked from the ruined garage door to the engine. "You weren't making it up, then?"

Cord walked out to the front door and opened it. "Come in. Who's your friend?"

"This is Razor," Colin said, stepping into the hall. "He's helping me."

The kitchen door opened and a woman looked out. "What is it, Sol?" she asked nervously.

"Wait here a minute," Cord said to Colin and Razor. He went into the kitchen and closed the door behind him.

"Maybe she doesn't know about his past," Colin whispered.

Razor said, "Or maybe we *have* got the wrong house and they're psychopaths and they're wondering which is the best way to kill us and hide the bodies."

Cord came back out into the hall, then opened another door. "In here, please." He showed them into a small but comfortable den. "Have a seat."

Colin and Razor collapsed onto a leather sofa.

"How far have you come?"

"From Jacksonville, Florida," Razor said. "We drove all night."

Solomon Cord nodded. "I can see that . . . And how much do *you* know about me?" he asked Razor.

"Is it true that you used to be—"

"—*in the army*," Colin interrupted. "That's right."

Cord lowered his voice and added, "My wife knows the truth, but my girls don't. And I don't *want* them to know, understood?"

"OK," Colin said. "Can you help us?"

"First, we have to lay down some ground rules. You do *not* mention my past in front of my family. Or anyone else. You do exactly what I say, when I say it. Got all that?"

Colin nodded.

"Good. Now, I've got a few calls to make—and then you can tell me everything."

A few minutes later, Cord returned to the den, where Colin and Razor were both already asleep.

He shook Colin awake. "You hungry?"

"Starving."

"OK. We'll leave your friend to sleep and I'll cook you some breakfast while you tell me what's happened."

Colin followed him into the kitchen and sat at the table while Cord worked at the cooker. "I asked my wife to take the girls out for breakfast, give us a chance to talk. Bacon and pancakes all right?"

"Great, thanks."

He took a carton of pancake mix out of the fridge. "So talk."

Colin wasn't sure where to begin. "Did you know Quantum?"

"Of course. He told me you would come."

"What?"

"The last time I saw him. He said something like, 'When the boy comes to you, you have to believe him. You won't want to, but you must.' And then he said, 'He will be strong. That's how you'll know.' I'd almost forgotten about that. I thought he was just rambling; he'd been acting strange for months. I was pretty sure he was losing his mind. Apparently he used to have visions." Cord shrugged. "Obviously they were true. So what does this have to do with him?"

"OK . . . After the attack on Ragnarök's battle-tank, where everyone lost their powers, my parents moved back home. They still kept in touch with Quantum and a couple of years later he moved there as well. Quantum's son is one of my best friends: Danny Cooper."

By the time Colin had related the entire story, he'd eaten his way through a stack of pancakes.

Solomon Cord sat opposite him, listening without comment

until Colin was finished, then said, "You don't know where they are?"

"No."

"And you don't even know who's behind all this?"

"Apart from Façade, no. I'm sure it can't be Ragnarök."

"We'll try to find out which plane your parents were put on, see if we can figure out where it was going." He scratched his chin. "One thing I am bothered about is that the people who were looking for you in Jacksonville will almost certainly have got my name and address from the woman at the shelter. They'll come here. They might even figure out who I used to be. If they don't already know."

"I'm sorry," Colin said.

"I don't have the resources I once had, Colin. I don't even have any of my old equipment anymore. I couldn't take the chance that some burglar would find the stuff, so I destroyed it. The only thing I can think of is to contact Max Dalton. He'll help. And I'll ask him to set up a safe house for my family." He sighed. "My wife will *not* be pleased, but she'll understand. We've always known that the past would catch up with us." Solomon leaned back and ran his hands over his shaved head. "I don't know how I'm going to explain this to the girls . . ."

"How come you never told them?"

"After the last battle with Ragnarök, some of us got together. Me, Apex, your folks, Impervia, the Daltons . . . a few of the others. We all agreed that we'd leave the past where it was. Well, Max and Roz and Josh didn't have any secret identities to hide behind, so they had to officially retire." He smiled. "You know what's funny? I always kind of thought that a couple of them looked down on me because I was the only one who didn't have superpowers. And after it happened, I was the only one who could still cut it as a superhero. I didn't lose anything."

"So why *did* you retire?"

"I was thirty-five. I'd been a superhero for eighteen years. I had a wife and kids I hardly ever saw. I decided I'd done my part." He pushed his chair back and stood up. "You look beat, Colin. There's a guest room out back. It's got a bed and a shower. Get some sleep. I'm guessing that you don't have a change of clothes, right? Leave your sweater and jeans outside the door, I'll put them in the wash."

"Thanks. What about Razor?"

"You trust him?"

"I do."

"We'll let him sleep. I'll wake you both as soon as I hear anything."

Someone shook Colin awake. He rolled over to see a teenage girl—presumably one of Solomon Cord's daughters—looking down at him.

Oh my God, Colin said to himself. *She's gorgeous!*

And then she smiled, showing an impressive collection of multicolored teeth: yellow, green, brown and black, and a couple of very chipped and broken incisors.

Colin couldn't help staring.

"Finally!" the girl said. "I thought you'd never wake up! My dad wants to speak to you." Her *S* sounds had a slight lisp to them.

"OK, thanks." He waited for her to leave so that he could get out of bed.

She looked at him expectantly. "Well?"

"Um . . ."

"Look, I don't know who you or your weird-looking friend are, but Dad said that I was to make sure you woke up and not to let you go back to sleep."

"My name's Colin."

"Is that so? I'm Stephanie. Now get out of bed."

"Stephanie, I'm kind of naked here."

She grinned. "Kind of naked? How can you be *kind of* naked? Either you *are* naked or you're not."

"Well, in that case I *am* naked."

"I know. I checked."

Colin jumped. "What!"

She laughed. "Relax. I'm kidding. Hold on—I'll send in Shaver with your clothes."

"You mean Razor."

"Whatever. The one who doesn't look like he's seen the business end of either in the past couple of years. Does he really think that long hair and a beard is a cool look? Doesn't he know that the grunge days are over? And who is he kidding with those tattoos all over his butt?"

"You *saw* his—?"

Stephanie raised her eyes and laughed again. "You're an easy target, Colin."

Someone went "Ahem!" very loudly. They turned to see Mrs. Cord standing in the doorway. "Your father asked you to wake him up, Stephanie. He never said, 'Do your best to embarrass the boy.'"

"Sorry, Mom."

"I notice you're still here."

Stephanie gave Colin a final grin—which he tried to avoid looking at—then Stephanie sidled her way past her mother.

"And take out those horrible things!"

She reached up to her mouth and removed the fake teeth, then flashed Colin a real smile. Her teeth were perfectly white and straight.

Shaking her head in bewilderment, Mrs. Cord followed her daughter out of the room. A couple of seconds later Razor entered.

"Come on," he said. "Time to go."

He tossed Colin's clothes on the bed.

"What time is it?"

"Eleven-thirty." He grinned. "Max Dalton is here. Amazing, isn't it? He's actually *here*! I've been reading about him all my life and he shook my hand! He said, 'How are you doing?' Like, y'know, we were old friends or something! You know how long it took him to get here from New York? About an hour."

"Is that fast?"

"Hell, yeah! He has this incredible superfast flying thing. Sort of a cross between a helicopter and a jet. He calls it a StratoTruck. Didn't you hear it landing on the street? It's amazing! I've never seen anything like it! Anyway, he wants to talk to you."

Razor sat on the end of the bed while Colin got dressed. "So you met Stephanie," Razor said. "She's pretty cool, isn't she?"

"I suppose."

"They're twins, you know that? Stephanie and Alia."

"What's Alia like, then?"

"Duh! Didn't I just say they're twins? They're both DDG. Only Alia's the sane one."

"What's DDG?"

"Drop-Dead Gorgeous." Razor turned around to face Colin. "You know, I still wasn't sure whether to believe you until Max turned up. He's got a whole team with him too. Me and Mrs. Cord and the girls are going to the safe house until it's over. And you too. They don't want you in any more danger."

Colin laced up his sneakers. "They're not leaving me behind."

"I told them you'd say that. And they said that you don't have a choice."

Colin stood up. "We'll see about that."

He followed Razor back to the den, which was now packed with people. There were at least eight large men, all dressed head-to-toe in black. Still standing in the doorway, Colin peered past them. He could just about see the top of Solomon's head.

Just inside the door, Stephanie and her sister were huddled together, whispering about something and clearly baffled as to what was going on. They stopped talking and stared at Colin as he entered.

Everyone else in the room also stopped talking and looked at him.

Then they stepped aside, making a pathway into the room.

Sitting on the leather sofa, looking right at Colin, was Max Dalton.

. . .

"Sit, please," Max said, indicating the chair opposite.

Colin swallowed and stepped into the room.

Very softly, without taking his eyes off Colin, Max said, "If Colin and I could have a few minutes . . . ?"

Everyone else quietly filed out of the room. Solomon was the last to leave. He winked at Colin and closed the door behind him.

Colin didn't know what to say.

Max Dalton looked just like he had on television a few nights previously, though—like his men—he was dressed all in black. This close, Colin could see that there was a touch of silver to his hair and there were deep lines on his forehead. There was also an old scar on his neck, just below his left ear.

Max broke the silence. "You've come a long way."

Colin nodded. "Yes, sir."

"The last time I saw you, you were about a year old. And now . . . Your parents should be proud of you, Colin. Very proud. I know I would be."

"Thank you."

"Solomon and your friend Razor told me everything you went through to get here. I couldn't have done that when I was your age." He grinned. "Hell, I'm not sure I could do it *now!*"

"Do you know who—?"

"—who has your parents and Danny Cooper? No. But we think we know where they are, or at least where they were taken. We'll get them back."

"I'm going with you."

"Solomon told me you'd say that. He wants you to stay here. Despite your great achievement, you don't have any experience in the field. Your powers are unreliable. It's going to be tough enough to extract your parents without having to look after you."

"I don't care," Colin said. "I'm going. Leave me behind if you want, but I'll find a way to follow you."

"And suppose we stop you from following?"

Colin stared at him. "They're my parents. They need me. *Nothing* is going to get in my way."

Max smiled. "Spoken like a true hero." He stood up. "That's what I wanted to hear. Let's go. We have a lot of work ahead of us."

"Colin, I'm not sure you're ready for this," Solomon Cord told him.

"But I'm the only one here who has—" Colin stopped when he realized that Cord's daughters were listening. "I'm the only one who can recognize the others."

"He has a point," Max said. "Besides, I've already agreed that he can come."

Cord said, "All right, Colin. But you do exactly what you're told, agreed?"

"I promise."

Max looked around at the other men. "All right. Let's move."

Colin followed them outside, where Max's sleek black aircraft was blocking the street.

It was smaller than the Chinook, but even more impressive. Instead of standard helicopter rotors, the vehicle had four large turbine engines—two at the front and two at the back—which looked like they could pivot to provide thrust as well as lift.

"Max had the police close off the roads so that the public wouldn't see exactly what was going on here," Solomon said.

"This is my fault," Colin said. "Sorry."

"Don't apologize for something like this, Colin. Me and your parents saved each other's lives dozens of times. I'm happy to extend that to the next generation of superhumans."

Colin turned to Razor. "What about you?"

"I'll be around," Razor said. "Max offered me a job. Said that he didn't trust me not to talk to the wrong people. After all this is over, I'm going to New York with him and his team." He lowered his voice and added, "Though I wouldn't mind hanging around here for a while. Give the girls a chance to get to know me."

For a second, Colin almost changed his mind about going with Solomon and the others. *No, that's crazy,* he said to himself. *I can't be thinking about girls at a time like this!* To change the subject, he said, "What's going to happen to Ritchie's car?"

Razor grinned. "Oh, I lied about that. We *did* steal it. Max said he'll arrange for it to be returned to the owner in Florida."

Solomon Cord said good-bye to his wife and daughters, then called, "Colin?"

"Good luck," Razor said. He tentatively held out his hand.

Colin shook it. "Thanks for everything. I hope I see you again."

"Me too." Razor grinned. "Man, this has been a weird couple of days!"

Colin felt a sudden, stomach-wrenching lurch as the StratoTruck soared into the air.

Sitting at the controls, Max glanced back at Colin. "All right, we can talk freely here. Any questions?"

"Where are we going?"

"We figured out the most likely transport they took and traced the jet's path to a small airfield in California. Our sources say that there's been a lot of copter activity a few miles from there. My guess is that they're holed up in an abandoned mine. The infrared satellite pictures show some unusual readings from one particular area, the site of a mine that was officially abandoned in 1881."

"You don't know who's behind everything?"

"No. But we do know that a few days ago someone was broken out of a top-secret prison in Nevada. Whoever was behind that was pretty clued-up; even *I* didn't know where the place was."

"So who was the prisoner?"

"The only name they had for him was Joseph. He was arrested during the mop-up after Ragnarök's battle-tank. They never found out anything about him."

Colin asked, "So did *everyone* survive that day?"

"No," Cord said. "Not everyone."

"But the rest of you lost your powers?"

Max nodded.

Colin said, "Well, this guy Joseph can't be the one who's in charge. He couldn't have organized everything from prison. So it must be someone else. I'm pretty sure it's not Façade. He was undercover for eleven years."

"What are our resources?" Solomon asked Max. "Did you manage to get in contact with any of the others? What about Josh and Roz?"

Max shook his head. "Roz is in South Africa and Josh is working on something for the Department of Defense. There's no way to contact either of them right now. They wouldn't be much help anyway. As Colin said, everyone's lost their powers. Right now, as far as we know, the only superpowered people on the whole planet are Colin and Daniel Cooper."

"And *my* powers aren't even reliable," Colin said.

"Right," Max said. "When we find them, we'll have to figure out a way into their base to get Daniel and Colin's parents out. Let's hope your superhearing returns by then, Colin, because we're going to need it."

29

"DANNY, YOU CAN'T KEEP US HERE FOR-
ever," Façade said. Along with the others, he was tied up, sitting
on the floor in the center of the examination room. For the past
three hours, there had been no activity from the soldiers outside.
Before that, they had made several unsuccessful attempts to
break into the room and overpower him. Each time they'd tried,
they'd barely made it past the door before discovering that their
weapons were suddenly empty or missing.

"I know that," Danny said. "Just give the order to free Colin's
parents and the girl. I'm not leaving them behind. Free them and
I'll let you go."

It was a stalemate. Danny knew it, but he couldn't see an alternative.

Rachel said, "Danny, in order to calibrate the machine we
need to run some tests on a superhuman. So we need either you
or the girl. Don't you know how important this is?" She looked
toward Joseph. "I thought you explained everything."

Joseph nodded. "I did," he said, his voice barely a whisper.
"I told him the truth." He slumped to the side and lay unmoving on the floor.

Danny laughed. "Oh please! How many movies have we seen
that trick in?"

"Damn it! I was afraid of that," Rachel said. "We've been
here too long. He's crashing."

"What are you talking about?" Danny asked.

"We've been dosing him with thiopentone sodium. A truth serum. It keeps him submissive."

"Why do you need him submissive?"

Façade said, "Danny, untie Rachel. She's a doctor. Joseph needs medical attention right *now*!"

Danny shook his head. "No."

"I swear, this is not a trick!"

"Why should I believe *you*?" Danny screamed.

They stared at him in silence.

Danny turned to Rachel. "Supposing that it *is* true . . . Why were you drugging him?"

Rachel said nothing.

Façade looked from Rachel down to Joseph, then up at Danny. "You want to know the truth? You want to know what they're really up to? I'll tell you."

"Shut the hell up, Façade!" Victor Cross cut in.

"What are *you* going to do about it, Cross?" To Danny, Façade said, "Joseph was brought here because of his visions: his prophecies. He saw you leading a war against the rest of the world. He saw a lot of other things too: just flashes, mostly, things he wasn't able to put into context. Things that have been giving him nightmares since even before you were born. When he was in prison, they kept him under a mild sedation to keep him calm. We broke him out because we want to know what those visions were. That's what the truth serum is for. It helps him to relax enough for him to describe—in detail— everything he saw. And now it's wearing off. Danny, you remember that documentary about drug users we watched a couple of months back?"

Danny nodded. "You're saying that Joseph is suffering from withdrawal symptoms?"

Rachel said, "Exactly. I have to check his breathing, circulation, reflexes and blood sugar. Then I'll know how to treat him."

Danny hesitated.

Façade said, "At the very least, let Rachel put him in the recovery position!"

"All right," Danny said. He reached down and untied Rachel's hands and feet. "Try anything, though, and you'll be sorry."

Doesn't this guy ever *get tired?* Renata wondered.

The guard had been on his feet for hours now, standing in the same position, his gun pointed at her. And he was *still* talking: "It's a fact that in every conflict, innocent people have suffered. It's not fair, you might say, but you'd be wrong."

Renata sighed. *Just my luck to get stuck with a henchman who thinks he's a philosopher.* Aloud, she said, "You think that it *is* fair that the innocent suffer?"

"No, that's not what I mean. You see . . ."

Renata held up her hands. "OK! OK! Stop! Now, listen carefully! I. Want. Something. To. *Eat!*"

The guard sighed. "Hold on." He unclipped his walkie-talkie and spoke into it. "This is Escher, level one. The girl is hungry. So am I, come to think of it."

"Hold tight, Escher," Davison's voice said. "Things are starting to happen in the examination room."

"Roger."

He clipped the walkie-talkie back onto his belt.

Renata pointed to the ground at his feet. "You dropped something."

He looked down.

Renata whipped the chair out from under her and threw it at him as hard as she could.

The soldier glanced up just as the chair hit him in the face.

At the same time, Renata was running forward. She knocked the gun from his hands, then lifted him up into the air and slammed him hard against the wall.

She let him go and he dropped to the floor.

Renata crouched over him. "Where are you keeping Energy and Titan?"

She felt something hard pressing against her stomach and glanced down to see that he had a second gun.

"Back away, or I shoot!"

"I can solidify faster than you can pull the trigger."

"Go ahead. If you're solid you can't move."

"If I'm solid the bullet will ricochet and hit you."

They stared at each other.

"So it's a draw," Renata said.

"No. You lose. You can't stay in that position forever."

Renata stepped back.

The guard got to his feet and kicked the chair back to her. "Sit down."

Reluctantly, Renata uprighted the chair and sat down.

The guard scooped up his other gun and resumed his old position. "So anyway. We were talking about whether the innocent have to suffer. See, what you don't understand is that . . ."

Renata groaned. *God, this is worse than being in school!*

"How are you doing now?" Danny asked Joseph as he retied Rachel's hands.

"Better, thank you. And clearer."

"Clearer?"

"The drugs were clouding my judgment."

Danny regarded him. "So whose side are you on now? Mine or theirs?"

"Nobody's side, Danny. And everybody's."

"Don't tell me you still think that you need to strip my powers. You still think I'm a threat?"

"Yes. Yes, you are."

Danny looked away in disgust. "God, that's crazy! I'm one of the good guys!"

Victor Cross said quietly, "How do you know?"

"What?"

"You don't know whether you're one of the good guys. You couldn't possibly know. You're too young."

Joseph said, "Danny, when I saw that vision of you, I knew that I couldn't just sit back and let it happen. I had to do something about it. All this came about as a result of that."

"If I'm such a threat to the world, wouldn't it have been *simpler* to just have killed me when I was a baby?"

Rachel said, "We had to be certain that your powers *would* develop. Just because your father had powers didn't mean that you would. It's not like we could test your blood or profile your DNA to see whether you were a carrier. That's not how it works. It does happen that the powers are passed on from one generation to the next, but it's certainly not guaranteed."

Joseph shifted around to face his son. "When I saw your future, I had to make that decision. Believe me, I didn't want to. I *really* didn't want to. I wanted to pretend that it wasn't going to happen, that everything would turn out all right. I was sure that I could come up with a better solution, but—" He frowned. "I can't remember now. Sometimes the past is like a page with the ink starting to run. I *know* that we talked about other ways, but the memories are blurred now. But one thing that's clear is the vision I had of you."

"So you're saying that it *will* happen? That I have no control over my own future? If that's the case, why did you even bother trying to do anything about it?"

"Because it *isn't* absolutely definite. It's not like the future is already there, waiting for us to catch up with it. What I saw is the most likely future. But it's one that we must do everything we can to prevent."

"Including killing your own son?"

Joseph turned away. "No. I don't want that. I never wanted that."

"Why did you even *bring* me here? If the machine can strip my powers no matter where I am on the planet, you didn't need me at all, did you?"

"We needed to know exactly how the powers worked before we could be certain that the power-damper would be effective."

"Why? Why not just give it a go and see what happens?"

Victor sighed and looked at Danny as though he was being remarkably stupid. "Because, you idiot, without you here to test it on, how would we *know* whether it had worked?"

Joseph suddenly sat up straighter. "Wait . . . This isn't right. I'm starting to remember something . . . I went to him, told him about the vision, and he said . . . he said that this was the best way. Not the only way. The best way. Why? Why did he say that? I don't know." He looked at Danny. "*I* said we'd have to watch you, train you carefully. But he told me that the best way was to strip everyone's powers. And I believed him. Why did I believe him?"

"Who are you talking about?" Danny asked.

Before his father could reply, Victor interrupted. "Danny, the important thing is that right now, right at this moment, *you* are holding a gun on a group of people who are completely powerless against you. You think that's the action of a good person?"

Danny shook his head. "No. We're in this mess because of what *you* did, not because of anything I've done. I am not to blame for this."

"You have to accept responsibility for your actions," Victor said.

"Just as you have to accept responsibility for *yours*. You kidnapped me; all I'm trying to do is help my friends. Now . . . tell your people to order their release, or I *will* start shooting. It's not like any of you are innocent."

Joseph said, "Oh God, I remember! Danny, listen to me!

First it was *him,* controlling me, persuading me that it should be done his way. And then he lost his powers like everyone else, and I was locked up." His breathing became ragged; sweat broke out on his forehead. "But the vision *was* real. Danny, billions of people are going to die! You've got to let us finish the machine! It'll take away your powers; then all this will be over. I wish to God that there was another way, but there isn't—not anymore! If you don't let us strip your powers, there will be a war like this world has never seen! Danny, I'm talking about the *end* of the *world*! You're going to be responsible for that! And I won't be there to stop you."

"What do you mean? Where will you be?"

"Please, just do as I ask!"

"No."

Joseph swallowed. "Danny . . . I've seen my own future. I remember now how it ends for me. When I was about your age, I saw the first glimpses of my death, but I wasn't able to understand it until now." He inhaled deeply, held it for a few seconds, then let it out. "Danny, if my vision was right, it's going to happen very soon. But we can avoid it if you put down the gun. That's all I ask, just put the gun down. You do that, I won't die, and maybe that means that the future *can* be changed. Maybe we can avert this whole thing."

Danny stared at him. "You think I'm going to *shoot* you? Is that what you saw in your vision of the future? All right. Let's change it, then."

Danny flipped the gun into the air and caught it by the barrel.

His father suddenly relaxed, his shoulders slumping forward.

"Oh, thank God! Now, put the gun down."

Danny unclipped the ammunition cartridge. "No need. See? It's empty. I couldn't possibly shoot you now. And in case you get any ideas, I can reload the gun faster than you can get to me."

His father stared at him, wild-eyed with fear. "No, Danny, there's more to it than that! The visions . . . Look, I don't care what happens to me. My time is over. You're the one who's going to make a difference. Put the gun down *now!*"

"You have to listen to him, Danny," Façade said. "I know you better than anybody here! I know you're not evil, I know you'll intend to use your powers only for good, but these things have a way of getting out of control!"

"Don't give me that crap, Façade. You're condemning me for things that will never happen. And *you* . . . Joseph . . . Quantum . . . whatever your real name is . . ." Danny crouched down in front of Joseph. "You judged me and found me guilty on the day I was *born!* You destroyed my life and all because of one vague vision of the future. Well, I've just changed one of your visions. How do you know the other one will come true? How do you know it wasn't just a dream?"

"It was real. It will happen, unless you let us help you."

"*Help* me? That's what you call it? Help?"

"Listen to me, son!"

Danny lashed out and struck Joseph across the face with the butt of the gun. "Don't call me that! I am *not* your son!"

Danny staggered back and stared. Joseph lay, unmoving, on the floor.

The others stared at him. Façade said, "Is he . . . ?"

"Danny, untie me! Let me check on him!" Rachel said.

Danny didn't move. *This isn't my fault!* They *put me in this position!*

He couldn't help thinking of the rock he'd thrown at the cavern wall; how it had appeared to him to move at an ordinary speed and how it had exploded when it hit the wall.

On the floor, the pool of blood around Joseph's body was beginning to spread.

30

DANNY DROPPED THE GUN. HE TURNED and ran from the room.

One of the guards outside made a grab for him, but even as Danny watched, the guard slowed down, became almost frozen.

He raced through the tunnels, dodging around soldiers and technicians, and came to the huge main doors.

They were closed—locked—and there was no other way out.

I've got to get out of here! Danny said to himself.

Danny pushed and thumped uselessly against one of the doors. *Damn it! Open, open, open!*

It was an accident. He can't be dead. It wasn't my fault. I'm trapped and I didn't mean to do it and he might be OK he might just be knocked out and . . .

Danny slumped against the door, collapsing to his knees, and fell forward onto his hands. His stomach lurched and he dry-retched; he wanted to throw up but his stomach was empty.

Oh God, please don't let this be happening!

A voice behind him called, "There he is!"

Danny turned his head to see Davison and four other soldiers rushing toward him, their weapons raised.

"Cooper! Do not move!" Davison called. "Lie flat on the ground, facedown, hands spread out!"

Danny got to his feet.

"Last warning!" Davison shouted. "Down on the ground! *Now!*"

"No," Danny said. "No. You do not order me around!"

He heard Davison mutter "Kneecaps" to his men.

The soldiers aimed their rifles and fired.

Danny gasped.

He saw the brief flashes of the rifles' muzzles, instinctively closed his eyes and jumped back against the door.

A sudden, brief wave of heat and pain passed through him, replaced almost instantly by a warm breeze and the smell of dusty air.

Danny opened his eyes, but instead of Davison and his men in the darkened cavern, all he could see was a bright gray and orange blur.

He blinked, refocused his eyes and realized that he was looking at the other side of the thick, rust-streaked metal door.

He was outside. Somehow he had passed *through* the door.

Danny didn't waste time wondering how he'd done it. He turned and ran.

Danny ran lightly across the uneven ground, the sun beating down on his bare back. He was moving at about sixty kilometers per hour; it was much slower than he *could* run, but he still wasn't sure that he was going in the right direction.

The desert was littered with car-sized boulders and drifts of pulverized rock. Ragged, parched-looking plants clung to the undulating, eroded hills and mesas.

The relief he'd felt at escaping was overwhelmed by the sense of guilt. Less than a minute after his escape, his powers had faded again. He'd collapsed to the ground, not even breathing hard. He'd turned about and headed back, and it was only then that he realized he had no idea where he was. For all he knew, he could have run halfway across the country.

And then a small black flying craft passed overhead. Somehow, Danny knew that it was heading for the mine. It disappeared over the horizon in seconds, but at least he had some idea of which way to go.

After what felt like hours of walking, his enhanced speed finally returned.

Now he was still lost, but at least he was moving fast.

Oh God help me, I killed him!

I didn't mean to do it.

I killed a man, and then I ran.

He should have told me! He was the one who could see into the future! He should have told me how he was going to die!

I left Colin's parents behind.

I killed my own father!

No, he betrayed me! He condemned me on the day I was born!

I shouldn't have hit him. If I hadn't hit him, he'd still be alive.

Then I wouldn't be a murderer.

No, it wasn't murder. It was an accident!

The sun baked down on the rocks, causing a heat-haze in front of him. The ground seemed to shift and shimmer, as though there were pools of water ahead.

He knew I was going to do it. He should have stopped me.

It wasn't his fault. They were drugging him.

Before that, they were controlling his mind.

Façade caused this. He pretended to be my father for eleven years!

No. I did it. It was me.

I killed a man and now I have to go back and rescue my friends.

And when I've done that, I'll turn myself in to the police. I'll explain everything.

They won't believe me. The others will lie. No, Façade won't lie. He'll try to help me. He's my dad.

He's not my dad. My real dad is Joseph. Was Joseph.

Danny slowed down and stopped. There was something about the shimmering air that was unsettling. Everything looked unreal, as though the world around him was slightly out of focus.

He blinked and shook his head vigorously. Through the haze, he could almost see something on the horizon ahead, something large and dark, but indistinct. As he concentrated, the dark object broke up into many smaller objects and Danny realized that they were people, dozens of them, mostly teenagers, dressed in black.

In seconds, they were all around him, rushing past, taking no notice of him. They cast no shadows and were translucent and silent.

Then one of the figures stopped right in front of him and Danny saw that it was himself, a little older, it seemed. Certainly more world-weary. His right arm had been replaced by something complex and mechanical.

His older self turned and looked around and Danny saw more figures approaching from the horizon. They marched together: an army.

The older Danny waited until the approaching army caught up with him. They had weapons: large, powerful-looking guns. One of them gave a signal, and as one, the soldiers aimed their weapons and fired.

Danny watched as his older self raised his mechanical arm

and the hail of bullets bounced harmlessly off an invisible shield.

Then the vision was gone. Danny was once again alone on the deserted plain.

Was that it? he wondered. *Was* that *the future that my father saw?*

He couldn't understand what the vision meant. *Who were the people he'd been running with? Why had they been running? Who was chasing them?*

Disturbed, he decided to press onward. He had to get back to the mine.

I'll get Colin's parents out. They'll know what to do next. And the girl that Victor mentioned. Whoever she is, I'll get her out too. And then I'll go to the police and tell them that I murdered my own father. I couldn't help it. My powers had faded. I didn't know they'd come back at the wrong moment!

Maybe they were right. I've already killed one man, even though I didn't mean to. Maybe that means that—somehow—I will *be responsible for starting a war.*

A war that will destroy the world.

31

COLIN'S ENHANCED HEARING RETURNED
shortly before the StratoTruck touched down near the mine
shaft's main entrance. "There're a lot of orders being shouted
about," he told Solomon Cord.

"Can you make out what they're saying?"

"It sounds like Façade. He's saying something about going
after Danny—that they need to find him." Colin grinned. "He
must have escaped."

"Good. That's one less to worry about. Anything about
your parents?"

"No, nothing."

At the controls, Max Dalton removed his helmet and ran his
fingers through his thinning gray hair. He climbed out of the
seat and went back to inspect his team. "All right, men. By the
numbers. No heroics. No noise. And no weapons-fire unless absolutely unavoidable. Single file. Keep low until we're inside,
then stick to the shadows. Solomon? You're rear, I'm point.
Colin, you stick right behind me. Any questions?"

"Colin should stay here. And someone should stay with
him," Solomon said.

"No. We can't spare anyone. He comes with us. It'll be safer
for him that way."

Colin sat up suddenly. "Whoa!"

"What is it?" Solomon asked.

"Someone's dead . . . A man. The girl is arguing with some-one called Victor about what to do with the body."

Max said to Colin, "Did you get his name?"

"No, they haven't mentioned it . . . Now the girl's just told Victor that she wants to speak to him privately . . . something about those nights they spent together. Oh." Colin blushed. "I probably shouldn't have listened to that."

Max said, "All right, we've heard enough . . . Let's move."

He led them from the craft. The men were all wearing full combat gear, which made Colin feel very conspicuous in his jeans and jumper.

The ground was uneven, but didn't provide much cover as they crawled toward the mine shaft's entrance. Max shuffled forward, then raised his binoculars. "Strange . . . no one on guard. The door's open. Whatever the hell happened, the whole operation is coming apart." He stood up. "We're not going to find much resistance."

Cautiously, they walked up to the entrance. "Hear anything, Colin?" Max whispered.

Colin shook his head. "There's no one on this level. There's a lot of arguing going on . . . Wait, I can hear my parents! My dad's been trying to force a door open . . . They must be locked up."

"Can you tell where they are?"

"No. Too many echoes. I can hear a lot of the soldiers talking to each other. I think they're getting ready to go AWOL."

"All right," Max said. "We're in the clear. Let's get this thing over with."

They moved swiftly and efficiently through the tunnels, checking each small cavern, until they encountered one unarmed soldier who was clearly making a run for it.

Solomon grabbed the man and pushed him face-first against the rough wall. "Name?"

"I don't have to tell you anything!"

Solomon took hold of the man's arm and pushed it up behind his back. *"Name?"*

"Aargh! Carmack!"

"Who's in charge here, Carmack?"

"Victor Cross! But he's taking orders from someone else. I don't know who!"

"Who else?"

"A girl called Rachel. And there's a guy. Façade, they call him."

"Why are you running? What happened here?"

"There's a . . . a ghost."

Solomon laughed. "A ghost."

"I swear! I was on guard one second, nothing around me, and suddenly I was on the ground and my weapon was gone. It's been happening all over. And the foreign kid, the one they brought in—one of the guys saw him jump backward through the main door without opening it! He just sort of melted through it. Then when we heard that Joseph was killed, everything just fell apart!"

"Joseph who?"

"I don't know. I think it's just a code name. They never told us his real name."

"Cross, Façade and the woman. Where are they?"

"Two levels down. There's a wide corridor off the main cavern."

Cord threw the soldier to the ground and signaled to two of the men. "Cuff him, gag him and take him with us. What do you think, Max?"

"I say we go right in. It doesn't sound like anyone's going to be putting up much of a fight." He checked that Carmack's cuffs and the makeshift gag on his mouth were secure, then hauled him to his feet. "You're going to show us the way, Carmack." To his own men, he said, "OK, people. Single file. Everyone stay in sight of the man in front. Weapons at the ready. Safeties on, until I say otherwise. We want to get through this with no casualties. Colin, you stick with Cord."

On the next level down, Colin grabbed Solomon's arm and pointed to a heavy steel door. "In there!" he whispered. "That's where my parents are!"

"You sure?"

"Positive," Colin said. "Can you pick the lock or something?"

Max came back to them. "No, wait. Colin, is there anyone else with them?"

"No, there's just the two of them."

"Then we leave them there for now. If this does turn into a bloodbath, they'll be safer there."

Colin said, "Max, what if something happens to us? We should let them out now."

"I take your point, Colin, but let's do this my way, OK?"

Colin paused. "No."

"You agreed to follow my orders."

"This one doesn't make any sense."

"Don't argue with me, boy!" Max barked. "I've been doing this since long before you were born."

He continued down the corridor, followed by his men.

Colin followed them, but was moving slowly enough for Solomon to catch up with him. "I think there's something going on here," he said quietly.

"What do you mean?"

"Max Dalton almost *never* appears in public, but now he's suddenly charging around like he's a superhero again. It doesn't make sense that he came here with such a small team, especially when he couldn't have known how many people he'd be up against. And so far we've met only one of them. He could be leading us into a trap!"

Solomon frowned.

Colin stopped walking and Solomon almost crashed into him. "Solomon, help me free my parents!"

"Colin—"

"I'm a fool! Façade wanted to capture me and Danny, but I got away. Now here I am walking right back to him! And Max didn't want me to wait in the StratoTruck!"

Solomon thought for a moment.

"OK . . . We go along with him for now. If his agenda really is to capture you, then they'll come after us, and there's no way we'd get the StratoTruck started before they caught us. If they don't know that *we* know, that's our edge."

Colin considered this and whispered, "It's not a very *sharp* edge."

"We've no other option right now."

Colin froze. "He's coming back."

Max ran silently up to them. "What's the problem?"

"Colin's just a little nervous," Solomon said.

"Sorry," said Colin.

"We can't leave you here, Colin. The only way out of this is through."

Colin swallowed. "All right."

Solomon and Colin followed Max back down through the tunnel, to the large cavern where the other men were waiting.

Max said, "Colin? Can you hear Façade's voice?"

"Yeah . . ." He pointed. "Down that corridor."

As they approached the door to the examination room, Façade came out, arguing with Rachel.

"I want out," Façade said. "Rachel, I'm not kidding. This has gone too far. Cross is mad. Did you know that he has his own people working on something that none of the others knew about?"

"That's bull, Façade! Victor would *never* betray us! He's—" She stopped when she saw Colin and the others.

Façade stared at them.

Solomon Cord raised his gun, aiming it directly at Façade's head. "Do something. Try and take my gun off me. Run. Grab a hostage. Do *something,* Façade. Please. Do something that'll give me an excuse to blow your head off right *now!*"

Façade ignored him, looking straight at Colin instead. "Well done, Colin," he said. "Not yet thirteen years old and you made it all the way across America."

He looked at Max Dalton. "Hello, Max."

Colin turned around.

Max Dalton had drawn his pistol and had the barrel pressed against Solomon's neck.

Solomon drew his second gun and was aiming it at Max's chest.

Max pulled out his own second pistol and aimed it at Colin.

"Not the kid," Façade said.

Max looked at him with contempt, then looked back at Solomon Cord.

"Drop your weapons, Cord," Max said.

"*You* drop yours," Solomon said.

"You're not Paragon anymore, Cord. You can't dodge a bullet. Especially not at this range."

"This is true. But then, *your* guns are empty. I removed the clips when you were on the StratoTruck."

Max considered this. "I'll give you eight out of ten for that one. You almost made me check."

"Worth a try."

"Drop your weapons or I'll kill the boy."

"He's a superhuman, Max. You willing to take the chance that *he* can't dodge a bullet?"

"I have the upper hand here, Solomon."

"How so?"

"There is a house on the outskirts of Richmond, Virginia. Your wife and daughters are there. They're being guarded by my people."

"You—" Solomon raised his gun to strike Max across the face, then thought better of it. He looked at Colin. "I'm sorry."

He lowered his weapons.

Max said, "Rachel, take the boy into the examination room. Check him over. So far, he's only shown signs of enhanced hearing and strength, but that's enough for what we need."

As the girl led Colin into the room, he heard Max say to Façade, "What's the situation here?"

"Joseph's dead. It was an accident. Danny freaked out, lost control."

"The boy's powers?"

"He's fast. *Extremely* fast."

"And now he's gone?"

Colin realized that the girl was talking to him and focused his attention on her. "What?"

"Please take off your sweater."

Colin shook his head. "No."

"I don't want to have to force you."

"First, tell me what's going on here."

The girl sighed. "Colin, please do as I ask."

"No."

"Very well." She reached out and pressed something against his arm. Colin jumped as a powerful electric shock coursed through his body. "You want another one?"

Reluctantly, Colin pulled off his sweater. "Who was Joseph?"

"Danny Cooper's real father. Lie down on the table, please."

Colin hesitated, then she showed him the shocker. "OK, OK!" He climbed onto the table and lay down. "Did *Danny* kill him?"

"He did."

"Oh God . . . How did it happen?"

"No more questions."

"Just one thing . . . Are *my* parents OK?"

"They're unharmed. And as long as you cooperate, they'll *remain* unharmed."

32

CAROLINE WAGNER JUMPED AS THE DOOR to the cell was unlocked. Earlier, there had been a lot of shouting outside, but apart from that, it had been hours since they'd seen or heard anyone.

Lying on the next bunk, Warren sat up.

As the door was pushed open, Warren leaped off the bunk, rolled across the ground and pulled it fully open. This was a trick he'd done once before, back when he'd had his powers. He'd been captured by Brawn and locked up. When one of the villain's henchmen had opened the door to check on him, he hadn't thought to look down. Warren had crashed into the man's legs and knocked him over, then made his escape.

This time, however, he found himself facing the barrel of a gun.

He looked up and smiled when he saw Max Dalton accompanied by three soldiers. Warren pushed himself to his feet. "So, the rescue team is here at last!"

Then he realized that Max wasn't lowering his gun and that the soldiers accompanying him were some of those he'd seen earlier. "You're part of this? What the hell is going on here, Dalton?"

"I'm taking you to see your son."

"Is he OK?" Caroline asked.

"For now, yes." Max turned to the soldiers. "Cuff them."

As they were escorted through the mine, Caroline asked, "Where's Danny?"

"I'm afraid that he's escaped."

"Good."

"Good? *Good?*" Max stopped walking. "I was told that Quantum had explained everything to you. Don't you understand how important it is that we recapture Danny?"

"Oh, he told us. And I think I even believe him. But it's wrong to condemn an innocent boy because of something that he *might* do."

"Danny Cooper is far from innocent," Max said. "He killed his father."

Warren and Caroline stared at him in silence, then Warren asked, "Which one? His real father, or the one who was masquerading as his father for the past eleven years?"

"His real father."

"How did it happen?"

"Danny's powers are now almost fully developed, but he hasn't learned how to control them. He's fast. He hit his father across the head with the butt of a gun. Apparently it was done in anger; I doubt that he intended any real harm, but what's done is done. He's murdered a man."

"I'm sure he can claim that it was self-defense," Caroline said. "You people had him held prisoner."

Max shrugged. "Perhaps." He resumed walking. "I'll take you to see Colin. We have a few things to discuss."

"What the hell have you *done* to him?" Caroline screamed.

Colin was in the examination room, hanging by his wrists

from cables tied to the ceiling, keeping his arms outstretched. He'd been stripped down to his jeans and his chest was covered in hundreds of electrodes. Wires leading from a computer console ended in a helmet on Colin's head, completely covering his face.

"The helmet is feeding white noise into his ears, to make sure that he can't listen to us," Max said. "And these cables . . . He wouldn't cooperate. They were the only way we could restrain him. Trust me, he's not in any pain. The tests we've done suggest that he's going to be strong, did you know that? Maybe even stronger than *you* were, Warren."

Warren said, "Max, get my son down and take all that crap off him, or I swear to God I'll make you pay."

"This is necessary. We're monitoring every square inch of him. We need to see the effect of the power-damper as it happens."

"Your machine is working?"

"Almost. The nucleus is operational, but we need to charge it. Unfortunately, without Joseph's knowledge we've run into some problems. We're trying to finish it by guesswork. This could take some time."

"And you're doing all this just because Quantum told you he had a vision of the future?" Caroline said.

"He'd had other visions and they all came true, except in the few cases where we were in a position to prevent them. I have no doubt that this one will prove to be accurate too. Unless we can complete the power-damper."

"It was you," Caroline said. "Wasn't it? You used your mind-controlling power on Quantum, made him agree with your decisions."

Max paused for a second before answering. "Yes. Quantum was unstable for a long time before Mystery Day. All those visions over the years had left him . . . confused. He was finding it hard to distinguish reality from fantasy. But you must understand: *he* came to *me*. He wanted me to help him control the visions, or at least his reactions to them."

"And you saw this as an opportunity to get rid of all of us?"

"No, not at all. Caroline, I could control some people, but not everyone. Not enough to save the world. The only way I could ensure that we wouldn't all die from some superhuman threat was to remove all the superhumans' powers."

"Even your own?" Warren asked.

"Yes, even my own. We're doing this because it *has* to be done. Danny Cooper will become one of the most powerful and dangerous men on this planet. He will recruit an army and wage war. It will be devastating. Billions will die in the war, and those few who survive will be left with a burned-out ruin of a planet. No food, the ecology destroyed, the seas poisoned. Whole cities consumed by fire. Plagues, radiation, famine . . . The survivors will *wish* that they'd died in the war. But we can prevent that. All we have to do is finish the power-damper."

"And Danny will be otherwise unharmed?"

"Of course," Max said. "Ragnarök's power-damper didn't do *us* any physical harm, did it? If you don't like this, Warren, then that's just tough. Remember, all this is *your* fault. The damage you did to Ragnarök's battle-tank was enough to destroy the first power-damper seconds after it was used. If it had remained active, Danny would never have developed his powers, and we wouldn't be in this situation. But this time, the machine *will* remain active. Forever. You have to agree that the removal of Danny's powers is a small price to pay for salvation."

Caroline bit her lip. "Warren . . . he could be right."

Her husband shook his head. "No. He's still condemning Danny before he's done anything."

Max said, "Danny's already killed a man, Warren."

Warren said nothing.

"I want to talk to Colin," Caroline said.

"I'm sorry, but that's just not possible."

"He'll calm down once he sees we're all right."

"I'm sorry, no." Max turned to Rachel. "Get the girl down here. If Colin doesn't stop struggling, we might have to completely sedate him. I'd rather have a conscious subject for the tests."

Rachel nodded and moved toward the door.

Max called after her, "And see if you can get someone to find out where Victor is!"

Rachel paused. "Wait . . . You haven't seen him?"

"No."

She frowned. "That's not good. The last time I saw him was shortly after Danny disappeared."

Victor Cross loaded the last of his emergency supplies into the back of the truck. "Hop on board, Laurie," he said.

The technician hesitated. "Mr. Cross . . . I really don't think that this is a good idea."

"You leave the thinking to me."

Laurie opened the passenger door and climbed in.

Victor got into the driver's seat. "All right . . . We've got food, water, weapons and ammunition. We've got this little gizmo," he said, pointing to the watch-sized device on his wrist, "and we have a little over five million dollars of Max's money. We're all set." He turned the ignition key and the truck rumbled into life.

Laurie stared at the miniature force field generator. "I thought you wanted that for Danny Cooper, to shield him against the power-damper."

"You thought wrong. This is for someone very special who really doesn't want to lose his superhuman abilities."

"But the others . . . Won't they tell Dalton what you've been doing?"

"No, they won't."

"How can you be sure?"

"Dead men don't tell tales, Laurie. And neither do dead women."

33

RENATA'S GUARD HAD BEEN SILENT FOR over half an hour. He'd finally stopped lecturing her about morality after she started agreeing with absolutely everything he said.

She smiled to herself. It was the same trick she and her little sister used when their mother was ranting about something.

I wonder where they are now, she asked herself. *It's been ten years. They might have moved. Dad's always talking about moving to Denver. Maybe after I went missing they decided to stay where they were, just in case I came home. Unless . . . unless they think that I'm dead! Oh God, I hope not! No, Max will have told them what happened to me. But they didn't even know I was a superhuman. In the newspaper article Max said that The High Command weren't at the last battle with Ragnarök. But they* were *there! Why would they lie about that? And why did Max say that Energy and Titan were dead?*

Renata jumped when the door to the room finally opened.

Another soldier stepped in. "We're to take her down to the lab," he told the guard.

They approached Renata, one standing on each side of her. "Come with us."

"What if I say no?"

"Then we'll carry you."

Renata stood up and walked toward the door.

"We know what you can do," the soldier said. "So you walk ahead of us at all times."

The door opened out onto a walkway above the main cavern. A long, narrow metal staircase led down to the ground.

Renata started down the stairs, then grabbed her leg. "Ow! Cramp! I was sitting in the same position for too long!"

She glanced around. Both of the men were right behind her.

If I turn solid, they'll just carry me. And if I'm in front of them, I can't disarm them. I could jump over the edge and turn solid before I hit the ground, but they'd just raise the alarm.

One of the soldiers prodded her in the shoulder with the barrel of his rifle. "Move!"

Renata stood up and stretched. "Give me a second." She turned around, stamping her foot. "That's better."

Now she was facing the soldiers, standing at the top of the stairway.

She put her hands out toward them, her wrists together. "Aren't you going to cuff me?"

Before they could respond, Renata grabbed hold of each of them and threw herself backward.

She turned solid.

The three of them crashed down the staircase.

Unmoving and invulnerable, the fall had no effect on Renata, but by the time they stopped falling, the soldiers were badly bruised and unconscious.

That is such a good trick!

She turned herself back to normal, got to her feet and ran.

Colin couldn't see or hear anything, but he could still feel pain. The cables cut into his skin where they were looped around his wrists. If his feet had been on the ground, he might have been able to jump high enough to loosen the cables. But as it was, his feet were dangling a meter above the floor.

At first, the woman—Rachel—had strapped him to the table, but he'd broken through the leather straps as though they were made of paper.

Rachel had used the shocker on him, set to full power, and when Colin recovered he found himself suspended from the ceiling.

Now, it was all he could do to remain conscious.

He tried to shift his weight to one arm and pull against the other cable, concentrate on flexing his muscles, but the noise blasting into his ears was too much of a distraction.

I need to go up. *If I can rise up just a little, I can slip my hands out of the loops.*

But there was no way up . . . unless he could swing himself back and forth; then maybe his feet would find something to push against. But he'd tried swinging before, and each time he'd been hit with the shocker.

Maybe I can pull myself up.

He twisted his right arm around so that his fingers were touching the cable, then grabbed hold of it.

He gave an experimental tug; his enhanced strength was still there. He was able to move upward by about a centimeter, but that only increased the tension on his other arm.

What else can I do? Maybe I can swing all the way around, get my wrists below me.

He tensed his stomach muscles, then raised his legs and let

them drop. He swung back and forth a little. Then he felt the shocker again, this time completely numbing his left leg.

Warren saw what his son was trying to do. He also saw the young woman rush over and press a small device against Colin's leg.

He tried to move forward, but two of Max's guards grabbed his arms and held him back. "Touch him again and you're dead!" Warren shouted.

Max looked at Warren as though he were nothing but an interesting lab specimen. "Warren, you're not in a position to threaten anyone. You're here as a courtesy. Remember that."

Façade strode into the room and up to Max. "Cross is gone. He was working on something in one of the smaller labs. Four assistants, handpicked. Three of them are dead. No sign of the other one. Whatever they were building is gone too."

Max swore. "Impossible! I've known him for years—he wouldn't betray me!"

"You obviously didn't know him as well as you thought you did," Façade said.

Max ignored the comment. "Any clue what he was working on?" he asked.

Façade shook his head. "No. His computers have been wiped clean and the paperwork was destroyed."

Rachel turned around. "Max? I think we have it. I think we're ready."

"You *think*?"

"Without Victor, we're not sure. All the defenses are ready to go online and the nucleus itself seems to be functioning according to the specs, but . . . there could be some problems. This one doesn't work exactly like Ragnarök's did. The effect will be localized. According to Victor's simulation, it'll have a range of about three miles, maybe four. Ragnarök's damper used a tachyon generator to give it an infinite range, but we can't get that working. Aside from that, we're pretty sure that it *will* work. Once you give the order, it'll take a couple of minutes to get up to speed. Though the defenses will be active immediately."

"A range of three or four miles is not good enough. The boy could be anywhere by now. I don't want to have to track him down."

Rachel said, "You know, we *can* boost the output, but it could be dangerous."

"In what way?"

"The chances are high that it will cause an irreversible neural overload."

"Meaning?"

"Meaning that it'll burn out Danny's brain, probably kill him." She glanced toward Colin. "Him too, and the girl. And not just them . . . Some normal people will be affected too. Maybe one in a hundred thousand will suffer a seizure of some kind. Most of them won't be fatal, but they'll be debilitating and permanent."

"That's out of the question," Façade said. "We're doing this to save innocent people, not kill them. Find another way."

Rachel shrugged. "There *is* no other way. If you want the power-damper to work on a greater range, you get the seizures too."

Max Dalton looked at Façade and Rachel. "One person out of every hundred thousand . . . That's about sixty thousand people throughout the world." He was silent for a few seconds, then said, "That's far fewer than will die in the war. Acceptable losses. Do it, Rachel. Do it now."

34

OUTSIDE THE ROOM, RENATA LISTENED with growing fear.

The nucleus . . . That has to be the huge silver ball in the lower cavern. But there's no way I can get to it, not if it still has that null-field around it.

She heard someone coming and ducked out of sight. Two soldiers passed by, one of them carrying a tray of food, the other checking through a set of keys.

Renata followed them at a distance and watched as the one with the keys drew his gun before unlocking a heavy steel door. The other soldier put the tray of food on the ground and used his foot to slide it into the room.

They locked the door behind them and moved on.

Another prisoner, Renata realized. Checking that there was no one around, she approached the door and knocked quietly on it. "Who's in there?"

After a pause, a faint voice said, "Who's out *there?*"

Renata kneeled down and put her face to the narrow gap under the door. "My name is Diamond."

Another pause. *"Diamond?"*

"That's right."

"Diamond, my name is Solomon Cord. You knew me as Paragon. I don't suppose they left the key in the lock?"

"No."

"OK. See if you can find something to get this door open."

Renata smiled. Paragon might remember her name, but he didn't seem to be able to remember what she could do. She pressed her hands flat against the surface of the door, then curled her fingers, pressing them into the metal. She tensed her muscles, pulled, and then—with a loud *crack*—the lock snapped.

She pulled the door open enough for Solomon to step through.

He stared at her. "Never thought I'd see *you* again. Thank you. Where are the others?"

"To be honest, I really don't know what's going on. Max is here. He's got Titan and Energy prisoner. And a boy, I think he's their son."

"He is. That's Colin. Where's the other boy? Where's Danny?"

"I don't know. Max has some machine called a power-damper. It's supposed to remove our superhuman powers. Is that possible?"

He nodded. "It's happened before."

"The woman—Rachel—said that there's something wrong with the machine. It'll almost certainly kill Colin and Danny and me, and probably cause fatal seizures in thousands of people!"

"Do you know where the machine is?"

"There's a huge room, way down on the lowest level. But it's protected by something called a null-field. I don't think there's a way to stop it."

"We'll stop it. We don't have a choice."

"Max, I'm *begging* you not to do this!"

"I'm sorry, Caroline. I really am. If there was another way,

I'd take it. Danny's already showing signs of being unstable. Before he escaped, we did some tests on his powers. He's incredibly dangerous."

"You're willing to sacrifice Colin and Danny and Diamond and thousands of other people just because of Quantum's prophecy?"

"Caroline, I don't do this lightly."

"What if one of your children was a superhuman? Would you sacrifice them just to remove a threat that might not happen?"

"Yes . . . yes, I would."

"Max, this is crazy," Façade said. "This is cold-blooded murder!"

Max turned on him. "You think I don't *know* that?" he yelled. "You think that this is *easy* for me? And do you think I'm ever going to be able to sleep again? Their deaths will be on my conscience for the rest of my life! But if I *don't* do it, I'll be allowing the deaths of billions of people!"

"*If* the war happens."

"It will happen! Quantum was right. You know that he foresaw much of what's transpired here today? He knew that he'd be killed by his own son. He also saw that a boy would make a difficult journey to find Solomon Cord."

"What else did he see?"

"Before the battle with Ragnarök we taped a lot of interviews with him, made after his visions. Most of what he said concerned the coming war. He said . . . there was a young girl, trapped in a ruined building, her leg pinned. She was starving to death. And at the same time, the *same* girl was outside the building, helping others to dig through the rubble. There was another one: an old man, desperately trying to defuse a powerful bomb . . . and failing."

"Look, did he say what causes the war to start? Maybe it happens because of what you're doing right now."

"Warren, we *have* thought of that. But I have to go ahead anyway. I have to do what's right."

"But this *isn't* right, Max," Caroline said. "You're willing to put innocent people to death. All those years we worked together, we were fighting on behalf of those who couldn't fight back. We were protecting the innocent."

Max looked at her. "Sometimes the innocent have to suffer for the greater good."

She glared at him. "Who are *you* to define the greater good? You're not God!"

He turned away from her and to Façade he said, "How long before the machine is fully charged?"

"A couple more minutes. Max, don't do this!"

Max Dalton shook his head. "You were a second-rate villain, Façade. It's a bit late now to be growing a conscience."

Façade started to respond, but Max held up his hand. "Wait, wait . . ." He signaled to one of his guards. "Take this man to one of the holding cells. He's served his purpose."

Façade backed away. "What? Wait a second!"

"If he tries anything, shoot to kill."

35

SOLOMON AND RENATA KEPT TO THE shadows as they made their way down to the power-damper's cavern.

"Left at the next turn, I think," Renata said.

"Quiet—someone's coming!" Cord looked around. There was no clear hiding place. "Hell. Diamond, we're going to have to face them. Turn yourself solid."

"What are you going to do?"

Cord grinned. "What I was *born* to do. You know any un-armed combat?"

"Not really, no."

"Then watch and learn."

Cord ran silently to the end of the corridor. He could hear footsteps.

Three people, he said to himself, *maybe four.*

The voices were louder now, loud enough for him to recognize Façade.

"I'm telling you, Davison," Façade said, "Dalton's gone over the edge. I thought that Victor was bad, but at least we knew where we stood with him."

"Shut up, Façade. I do what the senior officer tells me to do."

"That so? Well, Dalton's not an officer. He's a civilian."

"So are you."

Cord ran back to a doorway set into the wall, flattened himself against the door and peeked out.

Façade was approaching, followed by three soldiers. Façade's hands were clasped behind his head and the soldiers were clearly experienced at this sort of thing; they remained more than an arm's reach behind him.

Cord waited, unmoving, until Façade had almost reached him, then leaped out, knocking Façade to the ground and swinging his legs out to take down one of the soldiers.

He made a grab for the soldier's gun, but it was kicked aside.

He looked up to see the largest of the soldiers looking back at him.

"You must be Solomon Cord. Formerly known as Paragon." He looked around. "That was a nice move. You took down two at once. Stupid, though. I mean, Façade was clearly our prisoner. You should have left him alone. You're out of practice."

Solomon made a grab for the man's gun, but the soldier jumped back out of reach.

He slowly pushed himself to his feet and faced him. "You're pretty fast, boy."

"Faster than you, old man."

"Think you can take me?"

"I have an AK-47 here that says I can."

"How about putting the gun down?"

Davison laughed. "How about I put *you* down instead?"

His colleague said, "We don't have time for this, Davison! Just shoot him!"

"Shut up. Get Façade into a cell. I'll deal with this relic here."

Neither of them took their eyes off the other as the soldier dragged Façade to his feet and forced him down the corridor.

Davison said, "So . . . where do you want it? Head? Chest?"

"Just listen."

"You don't have anything to say that I want to hear."

"No, I mean, *listen.*"

From the far end of the corridor was a muffled thud, followed by a short, sharp scream.

Cord said, "That was your other man being taken out. Now the odds are in *my* favor."

"You'll notice that I still have a weapon aimed at your throat."

Cord took a deep breath and let it out slowly. Fear, he remembered. That was the key to this situation.

He stared at Davison. The soldier was taller than he was, though certainly not stronger. But he moved like a fighter and he was a good twenty years younger than Cord. Plus, *he* hadn't been retired for a decade.

"What's the matter, Cord? Having second thoughts?"

"No." He decided to try a trick that he'd once used on Rayboy. Cord held up his right hand, palm inward, and concentrated on it. He slowly closed it into a fist, then, just as slowly, moved his arm out to the right and pulled back a little, as though he were ready to strike.

Then, while Davison was watching this, Cord snatched out with his left hand and took the soldier's machine gun away.

Davison had just enough time to say, "What the—?" before Cord's right fist did what it was supposed to do and collided with his jaw.

Renata and Façade came running.

"That was good!" Façade said.

Cord turned the gun on him. "Tell me why I shouldn't kill you right now!"

"Because you need me, Cord," Façade said. "I might be able to find a way to shut the machine down."

Renata suddenly shouted, "Paragon!"

He whirled around to see that Davison had pulled out a handgun.

"I *said* you were out of practice, Cord. You should have frisked me." He angled the gun toward Façade. "And you . . . I was ordered to shoot you if you tried to escape. That's an order I'm happy to follow."

He pulled the trigger.

36

Danny Cooper walked around them, trying to figure out what to do.

Davison was lying on the ground, his gun aimed at Façade. The girl was leaning forward, her arms outstretched toward Façade, as though she was about to push him out of the way. The black man was in the act of raising his own gun toward Davison.

The bullet was now halfway between the gun and Façade. From Danny's speeded-up perception, the bullet would reach its target in about twenty seconds.

I can't push him out of the way, Danny thought. *At the speed I'm moving, that would do more damage than the bullet.*

He stepped close to the bullet. It was moving forward slowly and rotating.

He reached out and grabbed the bullet, then pulled his hand back immediately; it was too hot for him to touch.

I need something to deflect it.

Danny pulled the gun out of Davison's hand, then held the handgrip of the gun in front of the bullet.

The bullet pressed against the handgrip, slowly forcing the gun itself toward Façade.

Danny angled the gun a little and the bullet began to change direction. When he was sure that the bullet would miss Façade, he switched himself back to normal time.

Façade ducked as the bullet plowed into the wall above his head.

Davison stared at his hand, where his gun had been a second ago. "What the hell?"

Cord lashed out with the AK-47, cracking Davison across the jaw with it. "This time he really *is* unconscious."

"He missed?" Façade said. "How could he have missed? He was aiming right at me!"

"It was me," Danny said, appearing next to him. "I took his gun, used it to deflect the bullet."

Façade grabbed him. "Oh, thank God! You're all right! We didn't know what had happened to you!"

Danny pushed him away. "Don't touch me! I only saved your life because a shot in the head is too good for you! You don't get off that easily!"

"Save it," Cord said. "We're wasting time here. We have to shut the machine down."

"Follow me," Façade said.

"Someone has to free Colin's parents," Danny said.

Renata said, "I'll do it. I know where they are."

"What can you do?"

"I'm strong and I can make myself completely invulnerable. I can do it. You want me to free Colin too?"

"Colin is here? Then yes! Go!"

Caroline Wagner stared at her son, trying to think of a way to help him. She was the only one in the room who was watching Colin; the others, even the guards, were clustered on the far side of the room, focused on the computers that controlled the power-damper.

As she watched, Colin made another attempt to escape from the cables, but with no leverage he wasn't able to snap through them.

If he could at least see what he was doing, she thought, *he might have a chance.*

A movement at the door caught her attention; Caroline turned to see Diamond peeking in. No one else had noticed her.

Diamond stared at Caroline and mouthed the word, "Energy?"

Caroline nodded toward Colin and mouthed, "Help him!"

Somehow, Colin could sense other people in the room, but he couldn't hear or see them. He could feel their tension pressing down on him, like an approaching storm, and that tension was growing rapidly.

I have to act fast, he said to himself. *I have to get out of these cables.*

He concentrated all his strength on pulling himself up, but it was still no use. He took a deep breath and relaxed, ready to try again.

Then he felt a pair of hands grabbing him around the waist, effortlessly lifting him up.

Colin slipped his right hand from the loop of cable, then his left, and pulled the helmet off his head. He looked down to see a girl of about his own age holding him up.

She smiled at him and lowered him to the floor.

Colin started to ask the girl who she was, but stopped; this was not the right time for introductions.

He looked around the room. He saw Max Dalton talking to Rachel and his parents handcuffed. His father was watching Max intently.

His mother was the only one looking in his direction. She partly covered her mouth with her hands and whispered, "Can you hear me?"

Colin nodded.

Caroline Wagner gestured toward Max. "Finish this."

37

"THE NUCLEUS IS NOW FULLY CHARGED, sir," Rachel said. "Ready to go. Once we hit the button it'll take a few minutes to trigger the charge."

Max nodded. "Do it."

Rachel reached out toward the computer console, then hesitated. "Sir . . ."

"*You're* having an attack of conscience too?" Max pushed her aside. "I'll do it." He put his finger on the "Activate" button—

And suddenly found himself on the other side of the room, sprawled across the floor.

Colin stood over him, his fists clenched and his eyes blazing.

Behind him, Renata punched her fist right through the computer screen; it exploded in a shower of sparks.

Max coughed, a bubble of blood on his lips. "You're too late. It's started."

Colin reached down and grabbed hold of Max's shirt, lifting him easily into the air. Then he threw him back across the room, where he crashed heavily against the computer console.

The two remaining guards raised their weapons and suddenly found themselves facing Renata. "I wouldn't if I were you," she said.

As they watched, Renata's body shimmered, became transparent and glistening for a second, then returned to normal.

"You can't harm me," she said, "and the last thing we want

is bullets ricocheting around the room." With that, she reached out, grabbed the barrels of the rifles and pulled them out of the guards' hands.

Colin turned to Rachel. "How do I stop it?"

She began to back away from him. "It *can't* be stopped!"

"Where *is* the machine?"

Renata said, "I've seen it. It's on the lowest level. I'll take you."

"No, you stay here. Protect my parents." Colin grabbed Rachel's arm. "*You* can show me how to get there!" He ran from the room, dragging her behind him.

Solomon Cord stared at the silver ball that was floating in mid-air. "That's it? That's the power-damping machine?"

"That's it."

Danny looked around. "So how do we stop it?"

"This is how," Façade said. He walked over to a control panel set into the wall. He punched a code into the keypad. "All you have to do is . . . Hold on . . ."

He tried again. "Oh hell. It's locked out."

"Just pull the plug or something!" Danny shouted.

"It doesn't work like that! This thing is totally self-contained. It was built to stay online forever, just in case any other super-humans are born."

"Is there an override?" Solomon asked.

"No. There's no override. It's not designed to be shut down!"

"How long do we have?" Danny asked.

Façade pointed to a computer display. "Not long." The screen showed 00:02:54 and was counting down.

Solomon moved toward the silver ball, but Façade held him back. "Don't! Cord, get too close to that thing and it'll kill you! It's completely surrounded by a null-field."

Solomon said, "What the hell is a null-field?"

"It's like . . . a really thin layer where nothing can exist. If anything passes into the field, it just disappears."

They jumped as a siren sounded.

"Damn! The rest of the defenses have been triggered! Get out of here!"

Even as Façade spoke, Solomon could see several pieces of machinery sliding down from the ceiling, turning, aiming toward them.

Façade grabbed the others and pulled them toward the door. "Come on!"

They darted from the room and took cover in the corridor. "The guns have motion-tracking and heat-seeking features," Façade said. "Cord, they're rail-guns. Thirty-millimeter shells, depleted uranium tips."

"What's that mean?" Danny asked.

"It means that they're *much* faster than ordinary bullets—and much harder," Solomon said. "Danny, think you can outrun them?"

"I can try."

"It wouldn't do any good," Façade said. "Even if you dodge the defenses, you still wouldn't be able to get through the null-field! And even if you *could* somehow disable the null-field, the thing is spinning at a couple of million revs a second. *And* it's armor-plated."

With a deafening crash, something ripped its way through the ceiling of the corridor, showering them with plaster, dust and fist-sized chunks of concrete.

Amid the debris, Colin landed lightly on his feet.

Through the hole in the ceiling, the others could see Rachel peering down.

"That's it?" Colin asked, looking into the room.

Façade nodded. "We can't stop it. Can't even get to it."

"How long do we have?"

"One minute forty-seven. Colin, if you can get through the guns, there's a panel on the far wall that controls the guns' sensors. Destroy that and it should shut the guns down."

"I don't think I'm bulletproof," Colin said.

Danny said, "I know someone who *is* . . ." He took a deep breath and focused. So far, his superspeed had activated only by itself; he'd never been able to trigger it deliberately.

This time it has *to work.*

"No . . . It's no good. I can't go into slow-time!"

Cord reached out and slapped Danny hard across the back of the head.

Danny whirled around and glared at Cord. His burst of anger had done the trick; he was moving in slow-time again.

He ran back through the mine, back to the room in which Colin had been held prisoner.

He paused long enough to take in the scene; Colin's parents were now free of their handcuffs. His mother was holding a gun on the guards while his father crouched over Max Dalton. Renata was standing nearby.

Danny grabbed her, picked her up and ran.

Colin jumped. A second ago, Solomon Cord had hit Danny. Now, Danny was standing in a different place and the girl was next to him, looking confused.

Renata looked around. "What? How did—?"

"You said you can make yourself invulnerable, right? You're bulletproof?" Danny asked.

"Yes. When I'm in solid form. Why?"

"No time for questions! Do it! Now!"

Renata nodded and instantly became unmoving and transparent.

Colin understood exactly what Danny was suggesting; he picked up Diamond and rushed into the room, holding her in front of him as a shield.

Façade shouted after him, "Colin, just keep well clear of that silver ball!"

The noise was almost deafening; bullets rattled off Diamond's inert form, almost knocking her from his grasp.

Ahead, Colin saw the panel that Façade had mentioned. Still holding on to Diamond with his left hand, he clenched his right fist and pushed it through the panel.

Instantly, the bullet fire stopped and the others rushed into the room.

"Eighty-one seconds!" Façade said.

Colin looked around. "What next?"

Danny pointed to the machine's nucleus. "That thing . . . That's the heart of the machine. We need to disable it, but it's got a force field around it."

"No problem," Colin said, moving forward.

"No, wait!" Façade said. "It's not that simple . . . That force field can kill *anything*. Even you. You get closer than three meters and bits of you will just disappear. It's a null-field. It'll destroy any kind of matter."

Solomon Cord said softly, "Wait . . . We can see through the field. If it doesn't affect light, then maybe something moving at light-speed can get through. Danny?"

Danny stepped back. "No *way*! I can't move that fast!"

"You have to try, Dan," Façade said. "If you can get through, there's a small control box somewhere on the nucleus. Pull the cables and it'll deactivate the field."

"It'll kill me!"

Façade said, "Danny, if the machine activates, then you're dead anyway. And so are Colin and Diamond—and thousands of other people. You can do it, son. I have faith in you."

Colin turned to Danny. "He's right, Dan. You can do it."

The two friends looked at each other.

Danny swallowed. "All right." He forced a smile. "If I don't make it, you can have my bike."

He concentrated, switching himself into slow-time. The silver ball was now moving slowly enough that he could see its rotation. *I need to be* faster.

The ball slowed further and the room grew darker.

Oh great. If I'm moving faster than light, then I'm not going to be able to see!

He angled himself so that he was facing the nucleus and concentrated harder.

The ball stopped and everything went black.

Danny ran forward and stopped when he was sure he'd passed through the null-field.

He allowed himself to slow down a little . . . The light returned and he could see that the nucleus was directly in front of him, rotating. As he watched, a control box about the size of his hand rolled into view.

Danny reached out and pulled the cables from the box.

Is that it? Did it work?

He turned to the others and shifted back to normal time. They were all still looking at where he had been standing.

"It's done," he said.

They whirled around to look at him.

"You're sure?" Solomon asked.

Renata said, "Only one way to find out." She walked right up to Danny and smiled. "I'm not dead? Then it worked!"

"We're not done yet," Façade said. "We still have to destroy the nucleus!"

"*I'll* take care of that," Colin said. He rushed up to the silver ball and punched as hard as he could.

The nucleus was spinning so fast that his fist was knocked aside. "Uh-oh. How do we stop it from spinning?"

"The base," Façade said. "It generates a magnetic field to keep the nucleus levitated."

Colin slammed his fists through the base beneath the nucleus.

The huge silver ball slowed, wobbled, then, with a crash, dropped to its base and stopped spinning.

Solomon Cord raised his AK-47 and aimed it at the enormous, armored ball. "Everyone take cover!"

"That won't work, Cord," Façade said. "It can withstand almost any attack. That's reinforced titanium."

Colin scrambled onto the top of the nucleus and began to punch down.

"You'll never get through the casing!" Façade said.

Through gritted teeth, Colin said, "Oh yeah?"

He punched down as hard as he could, leaving a small but noticeable dent in the surface.

"Twenty-eight seconds," Façade said.

Colin punched again and again in the same spot. It was beginning to buckle, but slowly. Too slowly.

Solomon turned to Renata. "You have to help him, Diamond! Rip a hole in it or something!"

She stepped forward and pressed her hands against the nucleus's casing. As she had with the door to Solomon's cell, she curled her fingers into the metal and then pulled. "It's working!"

Colin jumped down next to her, grabbed the torn edge of the ball's armor plating and ripped it off.

There was another layer of armor underneath.

Diamond reached out again, but this time was unable to make even a dent in the armor. "I can't. Whatever this is, it's too tough for me."

Colin began to punch his way through the second layer.

"I'm sorry," Diamond said. "If we had more time, I could do it."

"Nineteen sec—" Façade suddenly turned to Danny. "More time? She's right! Danny! It's up to you, son! You have to shift Colin into another time frame! Slow everything down long enough for him to get through the casing!"

Danny nodded, moving into slow-time even as he did so.

He walked up to Colin, who was now punching at a tremendous rate, almost faster than even Danny could see.

Colin's fists silently pounded off the ball's titanium casing. Danny stood beside him.

How can I do this? he wondered. He put his hand on his friend's shoulder, hoping that in some way Colin would also find time slowing around him, but there was no noticeable effect.

He glanced toward the computer monitor. Eighteen seconds. Danny began to panic. *What can I do to help?*

Then, for the first time, he asked himself, *What would my father have done?*

Danny instinctively knew the answer: *He would have phased himself through the armor and disabled the nucleus from the* inside. *But how could I disable something as complex as this? I can barely wire a plug! And if I'm unsolid I won't be able to touch anything!*

And then Danny Cooper realized what he had to do.

He shifted back to normal time. Seventeen seconds remaining. "Colin! Stop! Get out of the way!"

Colin shook his head and continued pounding. "No! I'm nearly through!"

"You'll never make it!" He grabbed Colin's arms and pulled him back, throwing him away from the nucleus.

Then he turned his attention to the machine. *OK. I jumped through a solid metal door earlier—somehow—so I know that I can do this.*

He concentrated, willing his right arm to become unsolid and then, almost casually, his arm slipped in through the casing and into the machine itself.

"Three seconds!" Façade said.

Danny swallowed.

This is going to hurt.

He closed his eyes and concentrated.

His right arm became solid once more.

Pain tore through his entire body as his arm fused with the inner workings of the nucleus.

Danny Cooper screamed for a long, long time before he finally blacked out.

38

COLIN ENTERED THE CONTROL ROOM TO
see Rachel crouched over Max Dalton. The guards were handcuffed and lying facedown in one corner of the room, being
watched by Colin's parents.

Rachel looked up when she saw Colin approaching. She had
a walkie-talkie in her right hand. "We need to call for help. Max
is alive . . . I think he's broken a couple of ribs."

"Did I ask how he was?" Colin took hold of Rachel's arm
and pulled her to her feet. He took the walkie-talkie out of her
hand. "So you have medical training?"

"Yes."

"Go back down to the nucleus and see what you can do
for Danny."

"But Max—"

"Forget him." Colin pushed her toward the door. "Just go."
He turned to his father. "You'd better follow her, Dad. Danny's
in a bad way."

As his father ran out of the room, Colin's mother wrapped
her arms around him. "Oh, thank God you're all right!"

"Are *you* OK?"

"I am now. What happened?"

"Danny . . . He stopped the machine. He pushed his arm inside it, made his arm solid again."

"Oh my God."

"There was no other way." He paused. "Solomon says the arm will have to be amputated. So what do we do next?"

"I don't know. In the old days we used to contact Max. He always organized the cleanup of these things. We need to call in the authorities. And not just the local police—there used to be teams who specialized in investigating superhuman activities. Maybe Max's sister or brother will know how we go about doing that."

"I don't trust them. Not after what Max did."

"Right now, we might not have much of a choice."

Caroline Wagner followed her son down to the power-damper's room, where her husband and Rachel were examining Danny. She was stopped at the doorway by Façade. "Don't go in there, Caroline. Really. You don't want to see."

"Is he going to be OK?"

"I don't know. Warren says he'll live. Probably."

Caroline lashed out with her fist, slamming it into his face, knocking him to the ground. "This is your fault! *You* did this!"

Façade pushed himself to his feet, wiping at the blood that gushed from his nose. "I know. I'm sorry."

"Sorry isn't good enough, Façade! It's not *nearly* good enough!"

She moved toward him again, but Colin held her back. "Leave him, Mum. He helped us in the end."

"I only wanted what was best for Danny—for us all," Façade replied.

Caroline sighed and turned back to her son. "How's Diamond?"

"She's OK. Mum, who *is* she? How did she get here?"

From behind him, Renata said, "I was going to ask you the same thing." She walked over to Caroline. "Energy, what happened? When I woke up I found a newspaper. It said that after the battle with Ragnarök everyone disappeared."

"Ragnarök had a machine to strip all of our powers. You were still solid when he used it."

"The paper said that it was ten years ago, is that true?"

Caroline nodded.

"What about my family? Do they know what happened to me?"

"Diamond, no one knew who you were! We didn't know how to get in touch with them!"

"But *Max* knew. I told him everything about me."

Caroline Wagner let out a deep breath and gritted her teeth. "That man has a lot to pay for."

Solomon Cord came out of the room, saw Caroline and smiled. "Hello, stranger."

She hugged him. "It's been a long time, Sol. Thank you for everything."

Solomon patted Colin on the shoulder. "This is one brave kid you've raised."

"And yours? How are they?"

"Growing up fast."

They began to talk of how they'd spent the past ten years and Colin shook his head in dismay. *What is it about adults that enables them to switch into small-talk mode no matter how strange the situation is?*

He turned to the girl, Diamond. "And you are?"

"I'm exhausted, that's what I am. Who are you?"

"Colin. What's your real name?"

"Renata." She swallowed. "What am I going to do about my family? My friends? My little sister is eight years older than I am now! Colin, what am I going to *do*?"

"I don't know."

She looked over to Caroline and Solomon. "They all lost their powers?"

"Yeah. There are only three superhumans now. You, me and Danny. Me and Danny didn't lose our powers because when Ragnarök's machine was used they hadn't developed yet. They don't kick in until puberty."

"I see," Diamond said. "But . . . well, maybe I'm wrong about this, but surely there are others?"

"How can there be?"

"You were three years old when it happened, right?"

"Almost three."

"So what about all the *other* potential superhumans who were older than you?"

In the cab of the truck, Victor Cross switched off the walkie-talkie and tossed it out of the window. "Damn it! They destroyed the power-damper! You wait *years* for a superhuman to show up, then three come at once!"

Beside him, Laurie was driving. "So now what?"

Victor ripped the miniature force field generator from his wrist. "Now this thing is useless! All that work!"

"So who was it for?" Laurie asked. "You said it was for someone very special."

"It was. Me."

Laurie turned and stared at him. "You? You're a super-human too?"

Victor nodded. "I was ten years old when Ragnarök's power-damper was used. Two years later my abilities kicked in."

"What can you do?"

Victor tapped the side of his head with his index finger. "I can use this. My brain works faster and more efficiently than anyone else's."

"That was your plan? Build the power-damper and protect yourself, so that you'd be the only superhuman left in the world?"

"Exactly. We needed to test another superhuman in order to build the machine. The girl was useless, but when Danny Cooper's powers manifested, we knew we could use him."

"So you needed the superhumans so that you could strip their powers, but instead they used their powers to destroy the machine. That's ironic."

Victor closed his eyes and leaned back against the headrest. "On the positive side, the only person who knows enough about me to cause any trouble is Max, and he's out of commission. I suppose it could be worse."

Laurie snorted. "It *is* worse, for the others. You murdered them."

"In the big scheme of things, they're better off. Now they won't ever have to worry about being arrested, put on trial and imprisoned. And *I* won't have to worry about them squealing on me. So everyone's happy."

"Why did you let *me* live? Why didn't you put a bullet in my brain like you did with the others?"

"Oh, several reasons. Partly, it's because we've got a long way to go and I don't want to do all the driving myself. Partly, it's because I like intimidating you. But mostly because I'm going to need you. You're smarter than most people and a lot of fun to push around."

"Mr. Cross, you're a sick, twisted, *evil* . . ."

Victor raised his eyes. "Evil isn't an absolute, you should know that. Evil is an opinion. What's evil for you isn't necessarily evil for me."

"That much is obvious. You're a murderer."

"Yeah, I have realized that myself."

"What now?"

"Now I'm going to have to go with Plan B."

"And what's Plan B?"

"You don't need to know that, yet. Just drive."

Victor closed his eyes again.

He thought about Colin Wagner, Danny Cooper and the girl, whatever her name was. Together, they would make a very powerful team. Possibly too powerful for him to deal with.

He reminded himself that the true mark of genius is in finding the simplest solution to a problem, not the most complex one.

If the problem is that Danny and Colin and the girl will be too powerful if they team up, then the simplest solution is to separate them. Turn them against each other. Get one of them on my side.

Aloud, he said, "You know something, Mr. Laurie? I think I'm beginning to like you. You're not in my league—no one is—but you're still a smart man. You and I have a little work to do. We are going to build an evil empire."

He grinned. "You'll love it! Trust me."

Colin answered the front door to find Brian standing there, looking worried.

"Where *were* you?" Brian asked as Colin led him into the kitchen. "I've been calling around for ages and there was no sign of anyone. I didn't even think you were here now; where's your dad's car?"

"It's getting repaired," Colin lied.

"So where were you? None of your neighbors knew what happened either. Though there were some really weird stories going around."

"Like what?"

"Well, you know that funny little kid down the road? The one who eats worms?"

"Oh yeah. Peter wossname."

"He said that he saw you and your folks driving away like mad, being chased by a helicopter!"

Colin laughed. "Hah! Kids!"

"So? What's the story?"

"Dad won a competition. A week in Lanzarote. The thing is, he didn't tell us, because it was a surprise. It never occurred to him that I'd have to book a week off school."

"Well, you didn't miss much there. But did you hear about Danny?"

"No. What happened to him?"

Brian shook his head. "The poor guy . . . He was in an accident, lost his right arm."

"Oh my God! How did it happen?"

"He and his dad went out for a walk. The night after your party, it was, and they were hit by a car. They both ended up in hospital, both unconscious. Danny's mother was going out of her *mind* with worry. She had no idea what had happened to them. Danny's still in hospital—he should be out in a couple of days."

"What about his dad?"

"He got home yesterday morning. He said that Danny's doing OK, but it's going to be tough for him with only one arm. He said that Danny's afraid that everyone's going to treat him like some kind of freak." Brian shrugged. "It won't bother me."

"Me neither."

"Anyway, I can't stay. I was just passing on the off-chance that you were in. I'm going to visit Danny in the hospital tomorrow afternoon. You should come along. What a week, eh?" Brian walked down the hall toward the front door. "So you're back in school tomorrow, right?"

"Yep."

"Great! You can tell me all about Lanzarote."

Colin opened the door. "Sure."

"And you can show me the photos!"

Uh-oh, Colin said to himself. *Photos?*

Colin spent the rest of the afternoon writing letters. One addressed to Trish at the shelter in Jacksonville, saying that he was sorry he'd left without warning and that he was safe at home now. He asked her to thank the driver Gene and everyone else who had helped him.

He also wrote a letter to Razor, but posted it to Solomon, who had promised to pass it on.

The third letter he wrote to the couple he and Razor had defrauded at the gas station. He'd memorized their license plate number and Solomon had used his connections to find the couple's names and address. Colin put a hundred and fifty dollars in the envelope and thanked them for their help.

Then he found an old receipt in the pocket of his jeans and dialed the phone number on it.

A man answered. "Hello?"

"Can I speak to Marie, please?"

"Sorry, she's not here. Can I take a message?"

"Can you please tell her that Colin phoned? From the airport?"

"Colin phoned from the airport," the man said slowly, presumably writing it down.

"Er, no. It's just Colin. I *met* her at the airport. Can you tell her that I made it back home and everything is OK?"

"Sure."

"And tell her thanks for everything."

"No problem." The man said good-bye and hung up.

Colin had been about to ask him for the address, so that he could post Marie's ten dollars back to her, but at the last second he changed his mind.

He decided that he could ask her the next time he phoned.

That evening, Colin and his father made their way to Danny's flat.

Façade opened the door and nodded when he saw them. "Come in."

"We need to talk to you," Warren said, following him into the hall.

"I know. Danny's mother's at the hospital. She took Niall with her."

"What did you tell her?" Colin asked.

"That there was some business left over from the old days. Something we had to take care of. I *am* going to tell her everything, but right now she has enough on her mind."

"Right," Warren said, nodding. Then he reached out and grabbed Façade, slamming him against the wall. He leaned close. "You'd better consider yourself a very lucky man!"

Façade stared back at him.

Colin said, "Dad. Let him go."

Warren relaxed his grip and stepped back. "Damn it! You were one of my closest friends! And all that time . . . What the hell were you thinking?"

"Warren, take a minute to think about it, OK? I gave up my old life to *help* Danny! After you destroyed Ragnarök's power-damper, Dalton started saying that now there was only one way to be absolutely certain that Danny would never become a threat."

"He wanted to kill him," Colin said.

Façade nodded. "I couldn't let that happen. I'd already been masquerading as Paul Cooper for over a year. The real Paul—Quantum—was too dangerous, too unstable. He was *terrified* of what Danny might become. I was sure he would have done it. He would have killed Danny."

"How did he end up in prison?"

"Quantum knew too much about Max's plan and Max was afraid that he was unbalanced enough to talk. So he had him put out of the way until he was needed. The authorities didn't know Quantum's real identity, so when Max told them that he was one of the bad guys, they had no reason not to believe him."

"And how did Max recruit *you*?" Warren asked.

"He showed me a tape of Quantum talking about his vision."

"That was all it took?"

"*You* haven't seen it," Façade said. "I know how people work—I spent enough time *being* other people—when I saw that tape I knew that Quantum's vision was true. It scared the hell out of me." He looked at Colin. "I'm sorry, I truly am."

"You almost killed Colin and Danny, and thousands of innocent people, and you're *sorry*?"

"What else can I say?"

"You can promise that you're going to spend the rest of your life making it up to Danny."

"I know that he's not really my son, but I raised him. I love him just as much as I love Niall. I swear that I will make him proud of me again."

Colin and his father arrived at the hospital to find Danny's mother fretting about—straightening the blankets and fluffing up the pillows—and his little brother stretched out across the end of the bed reading a comic.

Seeing that Colin and Danny needed some time to talk, Warren offered to take Mrs. Cooper and Niall down to the cafeteria.

Danny and Colin watched them go, then Colin said, "So how's the injury?"

Danny raised the stump of his arm. "It hurts like hell, Col. I still can't believe it."

"I never got a chance to thank you, before they took us away for debriefing."

"That's OK . . . You did pretty good yourself."

"Me and Dad went to see Façade on the way here."

"How's he doing?"

"Do you care?"

Danny paused. "I know I shouldn't, after what he's done, but I do. But he genuinely believed that Max's plan was the right thing to do. He keeps saying 'Sorry' over and over. But I think he's glad to be back. He missed my mother, you know? Maybe after all those years of pretending to be her husband he really did fall in love with her. He missed Niall too, more than he thought he would."

"And what about what happened with . . . ?" Colin hesitated.

"Joseph?"

"Yeah."

"Dad said that Josh Dalton's sending over some top therapist from the States to talk to me. Apparently she used to specialize in working with superhumans. This isn't the first time that an accident like this has happened."

"Is your Mum upset about your arm?"

"Well, she keeps trying to pretend it's not that big a deal, you know? She thinks that if she doesn't show how upset she is, then I'll be more relaxed about it. They gave me a book . . ." Danny pointed to a slim spiral-bound book on his bedside table. "It's supposed to help me cope." He sighed. "I'll tell you something, Col . . . You never know how much you use both arms until you lose one of them. I keep reaching for things with it. My balance is all weird too. It takes me damn near half an hour to go to the toilet! And I can't tie my shoes. Did you ever try buttoning a shirt using only your left hand? It takes ages. I suppose the hardest part will be learning how to write again." He shook his head. "I can't believe I was so stupid."

"It wasn't stupid, Danny. It was the bravest thing I've ever seen."

"No, I mean I was stupid to use my *right* arm. I should have used my left!"

Colin could see that Danny was on the verge of tears. "Um . . . Want to change the subject?"

Danny swallowed and nodded. "Yeah. Talk about something positive."

"Solomon Cord is talking about coming over for a visit in a few weeks. He said he might be bringing his whole family."

"And that's good?"

"You haven't seen his twin daughters. They're DDG."

"What's that?"

"Drop-Dead Gorgeous. I swear, they're . . ." Colin couldn't help grinning. "Well, you'll see for yourself."

"What happened to Renata?"

"Solomon's looking after her for now. He's going to try to contact her family. That's going to be difficult for her."

"What about Max and the others?"

"They were all arrested, except Victor Cross. No one knows where he is. Max . . . He's in a prison hospital now. Twenty-four-hour guard. The doctors say that he was lucky he didn't break his back. The official story is that the FBI was after him for money laundering and tax evasion and he was trying to escape from them when he fell down a flight of stairs in his apartment."

"Good. So it's all covered up like nothing happened?"

Colin nodded. "Max was wrong, you know. He kept saying that superhumans were unnatural, that we aren't needed. We *are* needed. We have a duty to the human race."

"Even if some of them don't want us," Danny said.

"Right. Solomon was worried what might happen if word got out. The press would love it, you know? Superhuman activities for the first time in ten years. They'd find out who we are and none of us would be safe. But it's going to be OK. Josh said that the people he's working with are experts in covering up these things. No one will talk. It's all over."

Danny nodded, but he didn't say anything.

He knew that it was *not* all over.

He remembered walking through the desert, remembered the vision he had of himself leading an army.

In the vision, Danny's future self had a mechanical right arm.

J.Albert Adams
Academy Media Center

DATE DUE			

4084 131223

FIC
CAR

Carroll, Michael
Owen.

The awakening

J ALBERT ADAMS ACADEMY

309371 01444   24216A   0001